WHERE IS HENRY?

MURDER MYSTERY AND INTERNATIONAL CRIME

J D WILLIAMS

SWEETSPIRE **LITERATURE**
—— MANAGEMENT ——

OTHER BOOKS WRITTEN BY J.D. WILLIAMS

IN PURSUIT OF THE INNOCENT

COME TO BED WITH MOTHER

I WOULDN'T CHANGE A THING

"A TRILOGY OF CRIME"

THAILAND TRIANGLE - DETECTIVE

AND INTERNATIONAL CRIME

FULL CIRCLE- DETECTIVE AND INTERNATIONAL CRIME

"A TRILOGY OF SCIENCE FICTION"

THE PILGRIMS OF GLIESE - SCIENCE FICTION

END GAME - SCIENCE FICTION

DESTRUCTION OF THE ORION NEBULA - SCIENCE FICTION

LIST OF CHARACTERS;

JACK MORRISON -DETECTIVE

FRANK JACOBS – DETECTIVE

MARJORIE SWIFT – BLACK OP/CON ARTIST

HENRY/HARRY – PERVERT/SADIST/CON MAN

CARL KARLISSONE – SADIST/MURDERER/CON MAN

JAMES K.- CON ARTIST

MORTY - CROOKED LAWYER

JEBSON – FBI AGENT

SQUEALING PIG RESTAURANT – HANGOUT FOR STRANGE
PEOPLE

ACKNOWLEDGEMENT

WANT TO THANK MY WIFE AND FAMILY THAT ENCOURAGEMENT ME TO WRITE.

CHAPTER: ONE

*L*ieutenant Jake Morrison was sitting at his desk trying to complete paper work from a case he had just closed. When the Desk Sergeant called. "Lieutenant there is a possible "two six one Adam" at Fourth and Moore." Morrison," Who else is on the scene?" There is a female officer attending to the victim and an Ambulance is on the way." He slowly folded up his paper work and stuck it in his desk drawer, thinking. "I'll never get done at this rate."

When he arrived on the scene he looked around till he found Officer Sara Jones, "Were you able to question the victim?" Morrison queried. Officer Jones," Kind of she isn't lucid. Something about having to meet someone for a blind date, she was attacked and sexually assaulted. The street lights were conveniently out and it was pouring rain, so she wasn't able to give a description of her attacker."

Morrison asks, "any witnesses?". "Yea, there's an older man who lives in the apartment across the street. He heard a scream around One AM."

"Who found the victim?". "Delivery man found her face down in the street and from what I am told he started to scream like a little girl, running around like a looney, woke up the entire neighborhood." Morrison hollers at the onlookers, "Get the hell out of the crime scene, what do you think the yellow tape is for?" Morrison looks at Officer Jones, "Jones, you were first on the scene, this is the sixth assault this month and it appears the MO's are the same and all the women seem to have a similar story."

"They were all supposed to have a blind dates and the location was a dark street, lights not working and I don't believe in coincidences. My thought is we have a serial rapist a very clever one." Officer Jones, "I beat you to it Lieutenant I've already called the City Maintenance crew to check and see if the lights have been tampered with. They will be here in about thirty minutes". "I'm impressed, were you able to find any evidence in this downpour?". "Not so far I'll come back in the morning when the rain lets up." While they were talking the Ambulance crew placed the victim on a stretcher and covered her with a water proof blanket, before placing her in the Ambulance. They inserted an I-V in her arm, gave her a shot to ease her pain, Morrison thinks,"The son of a bitch who raped her broke her nose and from her shallow breathing cracked a couple of ribs, plus a head wound. It appears she put up quite a fight but was overpowered the mugger was much stronger."

He shook his head and turned to Officer Jones, "We have to find this prick before he kills somebody, Do me a favor stay with her till she gets to the hospital". "Yes sir", she climbed into the back of the Ambulance closing the doors and it drove away with sirens blaring.

Morrison was back in the office by eight the next morning. Standing in front of the evidence board in the squad room. The latest victim was still in a coma. She repeated a name over and over "HENRY, HENRY, HENRY" so the Police had monikered the perp, "Where in the Hell is Henry?", he kept staring at a blank space on the board where the attackers picture should be, "thinking your ass is mine!!"

At the hospital the young woman was cleaned up. They took a vaginal swab hoping to find semen or DNA, checked under her finger nails for evidence. Officer Jones had kept watch all night waiting for the patient to wake up. Her cell phone rang it was Lieutenant Morrison, good morning Lieutenant, "Is she awake". "No still in a coma, we found a material under her finger nails, it appears to be latex I think this guy was wearing some sort of a disguise". "That's why none of the victims can ID him, he's always changing his appearance. I'll be a son of a bitch. Maybe the lab can find out where the material originated."

"Have you been able to identify her?". "No they haven't been able to, she was found naked, no drivers license, purse, clothes or any thing to tell who she is." Jones replies, "Morrison," I put out an "All POINTS BULLETIN" a missing persons report sandy hair, blue eyes, five foot three, pretty little miss, the question is how have the victims been lured into meeting someone they never met in the middle of the night, in pouring rain?"

Morrison had a call from Officer Jones, "The crime scene was washed out. We picked up everything left at the scene, hopefully there is some DNA or blood splatter. I have a theory on why the attacker strips his victims, he's a souvenir collector likes to reminisce about the women he molests". "That makes sense I'm going to review all the files to see if I can connect the dots", Morrison replies.

CHAPTER: TWO

He looked in the mirror and smiled thinking, "That dumb broad fell for my bullshit, hook, line and sinker. This one was going to help me with my trouble finding women, she walked right into my trap. When I attempted to sedate her the stupid bitch fought back so I had to clock her to shut her up.

According to the morning paper she's in critical condition, I thought I might have killed her but apparently she's still breathing. Really don't care she was a good screw, bet she won't forget what a real man felt like."

He went to work attaching her underpants, and bra on backer boards. Musing to himself, "I'm running out of wall space to hang my trophies, this is fun, a few more, my walls will be filled with memories. I just hope my bro Jimmy doesn't see my latest trophies he will be pissed off. He thinks we have better things to do than screw around with women, my bro can be such a schmuck at times." There's a knock on the apartment door, Henry wonders, "Who in the hell is that?" BANG, BANG, "open up! It's your brother we have to talk." Henry, "Wait a second keep your shirt on."

Henry opens the apartment door, "What is your damned problem?, we weren't supposed to meet till Saturday is anything wrong?" His brother answers, "You ass hole did you rape that girl?, you know I have a mark all set up for Saturday afternoon. What were you thinking, can't you keep your dick in your pants at least till we make the score? What if they find DNA and place you at the scene of the crime? This entire deal goes down the drain, just because you need a piece of ass. Get yourself a hooker for a hundred dollars and get off that way."

"AW Jimbo don't be such a party pooper, you know I can't climax unless I hurt them, it gives me the feeling of power over them. I can't climax without my subject is in total submission the sound of them moaning in pain is almost more than I can bare." His brother Jimmy is silent standing with his head cocked with a look that says you are full of shit. Henry blurts out, "OK, OK, I promise no more till we get our score, I PROMISE." Jimmy, "But no more bullshit and stay away from your computer, the Police will be monitoring all the Emails looking for Henry. Meet me at the next street from the old broads house at ten Saturday morning, we have to make our move before her maid shows up at noon. So keep your dick in your pants and stay in this apartment till Saturday and for Gods sake clean yourself up we don't want to scare the old woman, understand?" Saturday at ten they meet a block from the house and go over the plan. Jimmy, "Remember you work for me and are helping me catalogue the pieces of art in her house, you call her upstairs because there is a question about one of the paintings. When she turns around to look at the painting break her neck and throw her down the stairs. Prior to that I will have her sign papers agreeing to give me the right to auction her antiques, in reality the papers will give me power of attorney over all of her property and bank accounts. Then I can dispose of her property as

I see fit, there is a body bag in the back of the truck." When they arrived at the house he backed the truck up to the garage door so the body can be disposed of with out any witnesses. Jimmy, "Our mark will disappear, she is going to take a long, long, vacation that will be eternal, so let's get to work!" Henry, "I hear you brother let's get on with it. I need a good meal after we complete the job, so be ready to spend a few dollars and I don't mean hamburgers."

Jimmy pulls into the driveway as Henry backs the truck against the garage doors. They walk to the front door Jimmy looks up, the brownstone has been well cared for, thinking, "I will sell it for at least a million dollars." He had met her at a local art action and promised to invest her money at fifteen percent she jumped at the chance to allow him to handle her savings. They walked to the door, Henry rang the bell, DING, DING. Miss Leo opened the door, "Come in, come in I have been waiting." Jimmy, "We will get to work immediately, Henry please start taking an inventory of Miss Leo's artwork and antiques. Miss Leo if you could follow me into your study. There are papers to be signed so I can set up a retirement fund that will keep you comfortable for the rest of your life", she walked into the study signed the papers, handing them back to Jimmy smiling, "Please lets get this done my maid will be here in a couple of hours and doesn't appreciate any one in her way". "Of course we will be out of your hair before noon." They walked into the hall entrance, Henry was standing at the top of the stairs, "Miss Leo could you please come up here? I have a question about one of your paintings." "Yes, young man be right there. This old body doesn't move as good as it used to."

She walks slowly up the stairs. Henry is getting aggravated, "She is slower than molasses I need to get this over with." She reached the top of the stairs turns to him and asks, "Which painting?" As Henry reaches for her, her foot slips when she turns to look at the painting he is pointing to, loses her footing and falls down the stairs landing with a loud crash in a heap at the bottom of the stairway, "OHHH MY GOD", she just lays their moaning.

"Jesus Jimmy, what do we do now?". "Keep your cool we don't have to do anything. She missed a step and fell. I like this scenario better. We place her in a nursing home I have her complete power of attorney. We can sell the house and drain the accounts while she is recuperating, all will be cool." He pulled out a syringe and gave her a shot of heroin in the arm.

Stood there smiling as she started to get high. "Call an Ambulance tell them an elderly woman fell down the steps and needs medical help. I know a Doctor who will do as I ask for a price, he will put her in a Nursing Home and keep her sedated. The last he knew the old lady was barely cognizant. The Doctor he had paid off had done his job and then some. It had cost him a few bucks but it was worth it, the brownstone had sold for a quick million and a half. She had two million more in stocks and bank accounts and a million in art. When everything was sold they split for the Mid West, Chicago sounded good.

Lieutenant Morrison sat at his desk reviewing the evidence the case had gone cold, thinking. "I have to interview the latest victim hopefully she will be able to remember something. The case is going no where. He called the front desk. "Sergeant can you find the location of our last rape victim and can she be interviewed?". "Will do Lieutenant" an hour later Morrison's desk phone rings, "Morrison here". "Boss she was transferred to a convalescent home in the suburbs. Her doctor said she needed time to heal physically and mentally. I emailed the Convalescent Home address and phone number to you." "Thanks Sarge greatly appreciated."

All of sudden he felt light headed, the pain in the back of his brain was more than he could stand. Morrison pulls open his left desk drawer, fetches a bottle of pain pills, looks around to see if anyone is looking, pours himself a water cup full of Bourbon and downs three pills. Sits back and lets the medicine slowly ease into his system the pain subsides.

"Damned war wounds, that shrapnel will be with me till the day I die."

Morrison dialed the Convalescent home, "May I speak to Miss Sarahs doctor this is Lieutenant Morrison I am handling her assault case and I want permission to question her". "Hold on please, this is Doctor Jefferson may I help you?" Morrison asked to interview Miss Sarahs. Doctor Jefferson, "I can let you question her for about thirty minutes. This afternoon at three is that good for you?". "Sounds good will be there."

CHAPTER: THREE

He gathered up the information he had on the rape cases and headed out hoping the latest victim could answer some questions that hopefully would shed light on this case. The drive to the Convalescent Home he mulled over all that had transpired in the last few months. There had been a number of rapes, all had the same MO the women were stripped of their clothes, battered and robbed, all of them had been out late at night. The prior victim kept mumbling the name "HENRY" she had a concussion and no memory of the attack. Her psychiatrist said, "She has a concussion and remembering the incident would be too damaging to her psyche, because of the brutality of the attack."

Hopefully the attack on this young woman would not trigger the same defensive response. He needed to have an eyewitness description of the attacker. In his gut he knew this perp had been in prison. Lieutenant Morrison pulled into the parking lot. There weren't any parking places except a few marked Private or Medical Staff only. "I'll park in one marked medical staff, what are they going to do give me a ticket?, I don't think so."

Morrison walked into the main lobby, walked to the desk showing his badge. "Could you please tell me what room Miss Sarahs is in?

by the way I had to park in a reserved space, so don't get JIGGY and have me towed. I would not be a happy camper."

"She is in room thirty five, please wait while I inform her Therapist to accompany you. The patient is still having some effects from her trauma, and officer I will make sure they do not tow your car."

While he waited for the Therapist, he was lost in deep thought when someone tapped him on the shoulder. He turned and there stood a very stately young woman five six, auburn hair, brown eyes with curves to die for, "Lord he thought I must be in Heaven. "Lieutenant Morrison, my name is Doctor Amelia Mc Millian if you would follow me we can visit the patient. You must not push her, she is just beginning to remember and I am afraid if you put too much pressure she may relapse." Morrison, "Ok, I understand we know her name but still haven't figured out where she's from. Have you been able to find out anymore about her. The creep who committed the assault removed all personal effects." He walked into her room she was sitting up and looked relaxed. She was recuperating from the attack, she looked much better from when he had first seen her. He walked to the side of her bed and introduced himself. "You probably don't recognize me, I am Lieutenant Morrison I have been trying to find the person who attacked you. If you don't mind answering a few questions about your assault", she answered, "I'll do my best." "It was raining and dark why were you in a questionable neighborhood at that hour, can you give a description of your assailant?". "Doctor could you please raise the head of my bed." She turned looking at Morrison, pointing to a pad and pencil. He picked up the pad and pencil handing it to her.

"Thank you Lieutenant, when I was assaulted he struck me in the face, and it is very painful for me to speak."

She began to write, "I met him over the internet claiming to be having trouble meeting women, we struck up friendship. I foolishly said I would meet him and introduce him to a few people in my group. His computer name was Henry, we were originally supposed to meet early in the afternoon, I had an emergency so I asked if we could meet later in the day. He agreed and texted me where we were to meet. I wasn't familiar with that neighborhood so I didn't think anything about the new location." Morrison, "Can you give me a description of this HENRY, your attacker, was he tall, thin, fat, how was he dressed, his hair color?" she answered, writing on the pad, "It was pretty dark the street lights were out, I would guess he was around six feet tall, a scar on his left cheek, deep voice, I couldn't see the color of his eyes or his hair color. That is all I can remember, before I could move he knocked me to the ground, cuffed me and was tearing my clothes off. When he hit me the second time I must have passed out because everything else is just a blur, what happened after that I don't know. When I opened my eyes I was on a stretcher being loaded into an ambulance."

Lieutenant Morrison thought to himself, "This prick is one shrewd bastard, I have questioned six women who were attacked and raped. They all give me a different description of their attacker but the "MO" is the same, so it has to be the same man or maybe there is two of them working together. All six say they met him on the internet and his call name is, "HENRY," He thanked her for her time and left, driving back he was thinking, "I'll have to wait to see if the lab has been able to identify the DNA on the mask, next I will have the computer Geeks set up an algorithm to see if we can track this creep down. I am still stymied as to why the victims all give us different descriptions of their attacker, I am missing something." Lieutenant Morrison sat in his Police Cruiser thinking about his next move, "the Press was going to have a field day. There is a serial rapist running amok in the streets and the police department is helpless to stop him." The Press just gloried in these juicy stories and loved throwing stones at the department.

He drove back to the station thinking, "I guess I'll go through all the files again, there must be some link in this mess I'm missing. My gut tells me there is only one predator but WHY, WHY … do all the victims give a different description of who attacked them? the only thing they have in common is they met some creep on the internet named, HENRY." Lieutenant Morrison drove back to his office and spent the rest of the evening reviewing the evidence. Called the Forensic Lab to see if they had any DNA matches, nothing. At midnight he stacked the files on his desk."Damned I'm hungry, there's a Diner open down the street a large T-Bone would taste good, washed down with a couple of brews."

CHAPTER: FOUR

NOCK, KNOCK, "Open up Henry". "Keep your shirt on Jimmy I'm coming". "Pack your bags brother we are on our way to Chicago I have made contact with an elderly couple living in the suburbs looking to invest in stocks and bonds. They are eighty years old, no relatives it will be an easy con." Henry says, "Jesus Jimmy! I was just getting my apartment fixed up with my souvenirs I don't want to move them."

"Look bone head burn all that shit or you will be putting us both in jail. I mean do it tonight. Keep that prick of yours in your pants till we get to Chicago it's a big city you can have all the fun you want when we get there."

Henry answers, "Be cool brother I hear you. I will be a good boy till the con is complete". "Henry I'm not your brother"

"I know but you saved my ass so you're as good as blood." "OK, OK but don't screw this up or I will personally cut you and you won't have a reason to rape anyone anymore."

When Jimmy left he stood there for a few minutes admiring the victims clothes hanging on the back wall. This sucked he was just getting into the rhythm of using the streets to his advantage. "I guess

Jimmy is right, burn all my precious art work." He slowly removed all of his keepsakes from the wall.

"I worked so hard for these just to burn them maybe I will keep a few to display in our new apartment."

The Police don't have a clue,"When I took the make up course in California I was trying to get a job in the film industry. I would look in the mirror and wonder who I really was, then there was the "3-D" computerized machines that would let you make any face you wished. It was mind boggling I wanted to make those prissy bitches in Hollywood regret that they made fun of me. I picked that little blond with her nose in the air, she looked like she was sniffing shit. She was my first I crafted a mask that would make me resemble a contorted cripple and wailed her on the back lot. She tried to scream but I chloroformed the bitch before she could cry out I dragged her into one of the storage buildings and had my way with her. When I was done left her naked. It felt so good to have power over the opposite sex. Never again would I sit in my apartment and shed tears over a woman belittling me.

That's where I met Jimmy he was taking the same course on make up for the Movie Industry, we became blood brothers. Jimmy, "Hey Henry you want to have a drink after today's class? know a bar around the corner where we can get a drink that won't cost you an arm and a leg. Tell you what I will buy the first round I have a proposition I would like to talk to you about, screw this Hollywood bullshit there is plenty of money to be made without kissing these peoples asses, what do you say you game to listen or what?"

Henry looked at him not saying anything wondering, "If he was just leading me on or maybe he was for real. What did a good-looking guy like Jimmy want with me? he sure as hell wasn't looking to put the make on me because I would gut him like a pig" finally Henry answered, "Yea OK, what bar and what time?" Jimmy, "Meet me at the Purple Frog tonight at six, we'll have a few drinks and maybe make a few bucks at the same time." Henry walked into the bar a little after six looked around and saw Jimmy sitting in the corner. He was having a real cozy chat with Marjorie the Owner, he saw her slip him a piece of paper, kissed him on the cheek and walked away.Henry thinking, "This guy is a real schmoozer."

"Jimmy how are you doing I see you are real friendly with the help". "Keep your cool Henry she feeds me info and I use it to make a few bucks. Sit down and we can talk as a matter a fact there is a hit I have set up for tonight."

You want in let me know? "We should make a few thousand for the nights work." Henry thinks, "What in the hell am I getting into?" without waiting answers, "OK when and where is the hit, and what are we doing? I don't go for knocking anyone off." Jimmy, "To score a cool grand, killing people isn't my game". "Don't worry just follow me my car is across the street that red Ford. We have to move fast or we will be late." Jimmy pulled up to a gated mansion, Jimmy handed Henry a paper with the Gate code. "Over the wall brother and let us in."

Henry scrambled over the wall dropped to the ground and found the gate controls, punched in the code the gate slowly opened. Jimmy drove through the gate and rolling down the car window Hollered to Henry, "Now hit close button, we don't want some nosey cop wondering why the gate is open."

He pulled around the back of the house and parked, there was another key pad on the back door Henry looked at Jimmy and shrugged his shoulders.

"Punch in WW117 wait ten seconds and open the door. The code automatically unlocks the door no key needed. When we enter look for a camera to your left and I will take care of the one down the hall. Here is a cover for the camera make sure your mask is secure, we don't need any one to recognize us, rock and roll."

Henry turned the knob the door swung open. He looked to his left and sure as hell there was a camera he ran to the camera placed the cover and duct taped it in place. Jimmy ran past him and completed the same task it took less than a minute to complete the mission.

They slowly traversed the hall till they came to a large study, Jimmy held his finger to his lips signaling to keep quiet, turned to the left entering the study. He hesitated for a moment and went directly to a tall bookcase removed a half a dozen books exposing a safe. Henry thought, "So this is what it is all about this dude Jimmy is a CAT BURGLAR." He could see Jimmy had the combination to the safe, that must be what the Owner had given him on the piece of paper, somehow she was privy to the security codes for the estate. Jimmy opened the safe it was crammed full of hundred dollar bills and jewelry that took his breath away. The haul must be worth thousands of dollars.

Jimmy, "Open the leather bag we brought just hold it and I will empty the contents of the safe into it. We have to move I figured 20 minutes in and out, and we are almost out of time."

He closed the safe, put back the books taking a look around to make sure nothing was out of place. As they were leaving adjusted the angle of the cameras so they wouldn't pickup their images and removed the covers. "Alright brother lets get the hell out of here. When I stop at the gate the code is the same, we need to work fast the owners will be back any minute the play they were at was over an hour ago." Every thing went like clock work Henry pushed the right buttons and they were on their way, Henry thinking, "What in the hell did we just do?" his adrenalin was just pumping he was on a high.

"Man, I could live this life what a rush and I made a couple of grand in a couple of hours."

CHAPTER: FIVE

*T*hey drove back to the bar, walked in nonchalantly. Jimmy looked around and motioned to the Owner who was behind the bar. Henry heard a loud CLICK as she undocked the office door. They headed straight to the back entering the rear office. Jimmy walked to the desk, emptied the leather bag on the desk and began to count the money putting it in piles of a thousand dollars each, spread out the jewelry pulled out a Jewelers LOUPE "magnifying glass" and began to peruse the gems,"OOHING and AAHING", What a haul this will get us out of California and then some.

"Henry you want to take a trip? We can live real nice till I set up another con I have this old lady back east believing I'm a Investment Consultant. We could take her for a million or two then move on. Think about it don't answer right away, OH, by the way I know you attacked that blond on the movie set. That's why I approached you for the heist I knew you were a scum bag from day one."

Henry started to deny it, then looking at Jimmy just standing there giving him a blank stare knew he had been caught with his balls in a ringer, wondered, "how in the hell did he know it was me?, alright you caught me but how? "there wasn't anyone in the storage shed I checked around three or four times before I entered and I had to make her pay she was a real bitch." Jimmy said, "I was already in the building upstairs looking for a prop. I saw her enter and then you entered in the disguise I figured you were up to no good, must say for your first time you were a pro specially with the chloroform, Jesus you must have had a raging boner you did her half a dozen times", Henry answered laughing,… "She was always making fun of my makeup artistry, belittling my stature and looks she had it coming, I never heard if she had called the cops and filed a complaint, I wonder why?"

"You dummy I took care of it, she was too humiliated to call the cops it would have ruined her image in Hollywood. I untied her, got her dressed and took her to my trailer and cleaned her up. She swore me to secrecy and I have been having a flip with her ever since. I saved your ass so take that to the bank, you owe me big time", Jimmy grinned.

Marjorie who had given them the info on how to break into the Mansion entered the office and walked to the desk looking at the pile of money and jewels spread over the desk. Marjorie, "Quite a haul, I knew that rich bastard had a pile of cash hidden away, I sucked him in by giving him the screwing of his life. His old lady was too uptight to to be a good lay. He said she would just lay there like a lump of dirt and kind of sniffed like she had to blow her nose. Then I got close to his bodyguard by giving him head, and conned him into giving me the codes to the estate, by promising him sex whenever he wanted." There was twenty thousand in cash laying on the desk, She picked up ten and after looking over the jewelry pocketed the three most expensive pieces.

Marjorie exclaims, "The rest is yours, I can fence your jewelry if you want for an extra ten percent, or what ever makes you happy."

Jimmy speaks up, "Hey… BITCH we took the risk of robbing the frigging place all you did was get the codes. Now put the money back on the desk or…" he started to pull a knife out of his coat pocket, "I will screw you up." Before he could use the knife she pulled a pistol and stuck it in Jimmy's face cocking the hammer. Marjorie the Owner answered in a horse voice, "I'm the one who laid down with that "OLD SLUG" he complained his wife lays like a corpse she never moves and is stiff when they have sex. No wonder, he has the moves of a decrepit old creep they are a matched pair, he made me sick."

"I screwed the owner and gave his body guard some head to get those codes, so don't tell me what you did."

Jimmy dropped the blade slowly into his pocket. Marjorie screamed, "LOOK ASSHOLES, backup and pick up the rest of the cash. The jewelry on the desk is mine. You morons get out or I will waste you. I should have known better than get mixed up with two losers." They turned slowly and exited the bar closing the door behind them.

"JESUS, JIMMY, I thought for a minute she was going to blow us away. Why in the hell did you try to cut her? you really screwed up a good thing". "I screwed up by being greedy. I misread her she is not someone to mess with. Won't make the same mistake again" Jimmy answers. Henry chuckles, "Well at least we have traveling money. We could stay around till we find another score." Jimmy, "Why don't you move in with me while I look for another sucker?" Henry packed up his meager belongings loaded them into his run down Chevy and headed to Jimmy's place, thinking, "He only gave me a thousand dollars out of the ten. He said it was needed to set up the next mark, so I guess I won't complain too much I'm at least getting free food and rent." Two weeks went by Henry was getting restless.

Jimmy, "It would be a matter of time before we could pull off the next scam and then they would get the hell out of Dodge." It was six in the morning and somebody was banging on the front door. Both of them were in bed Henry was sleeping on the first floor and Jimmy on the second. Henry was the first to wake. "What the hell, who is banging on the door?", he crawled out of bed put on a pair of pants, hollered, "If you have a package leave it on the porch, I have no time for this shit go away!" the Intruder answered, "Sorry this package has to be signed for I can come back later what time is good?"

Henry, "OK, OK wait till I unlock the door, I'll sign for it." He unlocks the door, it is kicked open knocking him senseless as his body is slammed against the wall. He is having trouble breathing he looks up and sees Jimmy at the top of the stairs waving a gun, "Henry get the fuck out of the line of fire those two apes work for our lady friend. They must be here to collect the ten grand, that bitch has no scruples."

Standing in the doorway is two very large apes and I mean large, both of them are armed with automatic pistols aimed at Jimmy. Henry calls up to Jimmy, "Just give him the money or we are both dead meat, Please Jimmy just give them the money."

Without saying a word he lowered his pistol and went back into his room and came out holding a paper sack and threw it down the stairs.

One of the gunmen walks over and picks up the bag, while the second gunman has his pistol trained on Jimmy. When the bag is opened there is a bright flash, it blows up in his face blinding both of the intruders, while they are still stunned, Jimmy fires from the hip, catches one of the men in the shoulder knocking him backward into the street. The second gunman, blinded and disoriented dropped his weapon. "Now asshole back out the door and take your friend with you and tell that bitch if she think's she can take what I've earned she is sadly mistaken. So be good boys and get the hell off of my porch." The gunman backed down the porch stairs with his partner, screaming, "We'll be back to you "MOTHER FUCKER" and the next time you'll be in cement shoes." They climbed into their car driving off with tires screaming.

Henry crawled up the wall and limped over to close and lock the door. Jimmy hollered to Henry, "Get your shit packed we have maybe half an hour before all hell breaks loose. I sure underestimated that crazy bitch. Leave everything but your clothes and anything we can hock." In twenty minutes they were heading north. "I figured we don't stop for two days by then we will be out of their reach when we are out of California, when we get to the desert head East, we don't stop till we reach New York. There are real rich pickings in the Eastern Suburbs."

CHAPTER: SIX

They drove day and night, switching drivers every eight hours it took just a little over two days when they pulled into a hotel in Long Island. Jimmy,"Before we do anything I need to dump this car. I know somebody locally where we can trade this car in for something a little less conspicuous, then we rent a room so we can relax for a few days."

Jimmy drives to a Chop Shop on a back road parks, gets out of the car walks to the garage and bangs on the door, "Come on Frank you owe me. I don't want the money you owe me I want to trade my car for another one so we won't be recognized." There's a loud creak as the door slowly opens and this Grease Monkey sticks his head out.

Frank, "It is you Jimmy you thieving bastard. I thought you were in jail doing ten to twenty and they threw away the key, by the way who's your friend?"

Jimmy answers, "He's a friend of mine you don't have to know who he is. We just pulled a heist together and while setting up a customer we were rudely interrupted so to speak. Had to come East the weather was getting too hot out West if you know what I mean."

Frank answered, "I have just the car you are looking for. It has just a little more than thirty thousand miles on the speedometer, the boys brought it in last night, I just repainted it but the paint needs to be baked. I'll call you in the morning. Where are you staying I'll bring it to your Motel when it's ready."

Jimmy laughs, "Frank you're a real scum bag I could screw you up here and now. The car is painted put it in the oven now and we will wait for it. If you try to screw with me I will put a cap in your bald head then drop you in the Sound. You owe me from before, so pay up, if the boys come looking you haven't seen us. If I find you squealed your end won't be pleasant." Jimmy says while being up in his face" Frank smiles, "Ok, Ok, Look I was just kidding, the car will be ready in a couple of hours. Why don't we go to the nearest bar and have a few beers and relax?" At two in the morning the car was ready to go, Frank, "Here's the keys Jimmy, now we are even right?" Jimmy, "You squeal on us Frank and I will come back kill your wife and kids. Then I'll take you out and burn the garage around your head if you get my drift, so if you open you'r mouth they will find you in a barrel of lye." They climbed into the car Jimmy was driving.

"Were heading for the Ferry" Henry asked, "I thought we rented a room for tonight?". "I don't trust Frank and I really don't want to waste his family. He was my roommate in Prison and he was a snitch in the slammer, I would bet he still is. Frank rats to the cops. That's why they look the other way, he gives them leads so he stays in the Chop Shop business." Jimmy crossed over the bridge into New Jersey and turned south down the Turnpike. Henry, "I thought we're going to New York?". "Relax Henry, just being safe tomorrow I'll take us to the mark. I have to produce or my ass will be hanging out." Henry, "I thought it was just the two of us?". "Sorry Henry I owe the LA mob big time, we live on what I can skim the rest goes to pay down my marker." Henry just thinking. Jimmy pulled the car over, pulled a snub nosed thirty two pistol, sticking it in Henry's face. "You in or out,I can't afford you trying any bullshit. Follow my lead or get out of the car, now!". "Holy Shit Jimmy calm down. I'm on your side brother, whatever you say goes, cool it lets rent a room and relax like you said we have another mark to bleed." Jimmy uncocked the pistol, laying it between his legs. "Sorry Brother, just under stress, too many people breathing down my neck." They drove to the nearest Motel and rented a room for the night. Henry bought a couple of six packs and they relaxed for the night.

CHAPTER: SEVEN

Lieutenant Morrison was doing his usual drive around. It let him concentrate on a case when he was trying to put the missing pieces of the puzzle together. He would drive around at three in the morning. After an hour or so he took a break and stopped at a late Night Club that stayed open till six in the morning, sat at the bar and ordered,"Barkeep a shot of whiskey and a beer". "Be right up boss", Morrison asks, "Is the owner around?" Bartender, "Yes she's in the back. Who should I say wants to see her?". "Just say Morrison is asking" the bartender picks up a phone at the bar, "hey Maggie there's some guy named Morrison wants to talk to you." There was silence for a second, "Send him in I'll open the door" there was a loud… CLICK and the office door opened. Maggie called out, "Come in my friend haven't seen you in a couple of months, what's up?" Morrison entered the office walked over and gave Maggie a hug, "Missed you too, I have a problem, I thought maybe a second pair of eyes would help."

Maggie was in her forty's was a nice skate, still had a hell of a shape, to top it off, she was a good person to bounce ideas off of. Morrison started, "Are you aware of the serial rapist we have running rampant around the city, for the last six months?" we can't get a good description from the victims. Every victim has a different description of their attacker he's tall, he's short, he has brown hair, he has blond hair all the victims are stripped naked like he's keeping mementoes. Cons them into meeting him in out of the way places. A FIRST DEGREE predator."

Maggie thinks for a moment before answering, "I'm no psychologist but this creep was abused as a child either sexually or mentally he is acting out. Do you have any DNA or physical evidence?, after six attacks he must have left something behind." Morrison answers, "We have DNA but we can't find a match to anyone in our data base, OH YEA, one of the women had something under her fingernails, it appears to be some type of silicone I know it is a clue as to who the attacker is but the meaning escapes me" Maggie, "Do you have it with you? let me see it I may be able to give you an idea about where it fits in this scenario."

Morrison reaches into his pocket and produces a tagged Evidence Bag (of course this was totally illegal) to carry around evidence, but he was a BLOOD HOUND living and breathing his cases, handed it too Maggie. "See what you can make of this it's from the scrapings under her fingernails". "Maggie slowly turned over the scraping," I would say it looks like a manmade skin from a mask. It would take a professional to make a reproduction so lifelike that would be able to fool everyone?" "WAIT, I bet this Perp went to a school that teaches professional makeup. There are only one or two in the country where they teach this technique along with makeup. They have three-D computers that you can feed someones facials into and it will recreate that persons face. One of the schools is in Hollywood and the other is in New York City." Morrison, "I'll be a son of a bitch, how in the hell did I miss that. That's been nagging me for a couple of weeks, you are correct there are two locations for this type of training one on the West Coast and one on the East Coast… I love you Maggie I owe you one!"

He downed his shot, gulped down the beer paid his tab. Put on his coat and ran out of the Club, thinking to himself, "I knew there was something fishy about the witnesses giving totally different description of their assailant the bastard wore a new disguise every time he committed an assault. Morrison, "I'll wait till morning, contact the Makeup School in Hollywood for a list of students who have graduated in the last two years.

"Have one of the other Detectives call the school in New York and get a list of graduates," Hopefully there will be someone called "Henry." Morrison could feel it in his bones he was about to crack the case of the Serial Rapist. Looking at his watch it was three in the morning, he sets his watch alarm for eight o'clock in the morning that will give him time to clean up before he gets on the phone with the school in Hollywood.

RING, RING, his desk phone, "Who is calling me at this time of the night?" looks at the phone, "Shit it's my ex wife what in the hell does she want?" picks up the phone, "You know what time it is, what do you want?" She answers, "You are a dumb ass. Your daughter had her recital tonight you didn't even call to ask how your she did."

"She waited up till a couple of minutes ago waiting for her dear father to give her congratulations, where in the hell is your frigging brain? that's why I divorced you. You live and breath that damned Police force I couldn't take it anymore. You better call her in the morning or I will come down there personally and put my foot in your ASS" there was a loud… CLICK… as his ex wife slammed down the phone.

Morrison looks at the phone thinking, "There I go again screwing things up I should have been there for my daughter but no I have a case to solve." he looked at his watch, "Shit it's four O'clock I need a couple hours of shut eye. When I wake up I'll give her a call."

BUZZ, BUZZ, BUZZ, Morrison jumps up, "What the?? OH! yea my alarm I better call my daughter before she goes to school or my ex will have my head, he dials his daughter's cell phone, she picks up on the first ring, "Daddy, Daddy I got first prize". "Sorry I wasn't there last night I will send you flowers to celebrate. Daddy will definitely be at your next concert, daddy loves you."

She was sobbing on the other end, "Don't cry baby the flowers will cheer you up, Love you baby tell your mother I said hi", he hung up. Sits carefully at his desk, clicks on his computer and looks up the phone number for the school.

There it is they don't open till nine looks at his watch it's a couple of minutes before nine. At nine he dials the number for the Makeup School the phone rings a couple of times and somebody answers. "Hello, the best of the best can I help you? If you wish to sign up please go on line and sign up on our email. If you have any questions please dial zero,Morrison is fuming.

"This bullshit drives me nuts, dial this, dial that you never get to talk to a human being. OK, OK I will play your game I am going to dial zero I better get to talk to a real person or I will piss in the phone". "Hello may I help you?". "Yes my name is Lieutenant Morrison I would like to speak to someone in charge I need a list of your students for the last two years". "Please wait a second I will get my supervisor." there is a pause, "Hello, may I help you, who did you say you are, where are you calling from?"

CHAPTER: EIGHT

"*I*'m Lieutenant Morrison from the LA Police Department investigating a criminal matter I need a list of your students from the last two years, this is a Police matter."

"Sorry but that information is confidential we will need to see a warrant, proof that you are who you say you are please call back when you have fulfilled those qualifications" they hung up.

"What the shit, who in the hell does she think she is, hey George get me the Judge's phone number I need a search warrant."

George the legal Council, "What is this about I have to give the Judge a reason?" Morrison, "I need to have the LA Makeup Studio release their student records. I believe our Serial Rapist is a graduate of the school, that won't happen unless I have a search warrant. I want to catch this guy before he strikes again". "Hear you Morrison will get right on it." George, "I know someone at the school that may be able to give you the information on the QT if the Judge won't issue a search warrant." George, "Morrison the Judge said you don't have enough proof for him to issue a warrant, want me to use the backdoor?". "Do whatever I need that list". "Will do it will take a couple of hours." While Morrison waited he checked the computer and scanned the Dating Sites for someone named HENRY. There were about a dozen hits. He checked them out one by one no one fit the profile. Two were teenagers, one was a ninety year old man, five appeared to be abandoned sites that couldn't be traced the rest were lovers of a different color, he was at a dead end, thinking, "There must be someway to track this Schmuck. I want to take him down real, real hard put him away for twenty years where he will be made love to by a big hairy cellmate I would even supply the "KY Jelly." This creep likes to beat women I will fix that permanently when he is in custody."

Morrison's phone rang, "Hello, who is this?". "It's Sammy boss I have checked out every student at the school on the East Coast, "NO LUCK". They all check out none of the students have records, plus get this they are all women so our prep is definitely from the school in California."

Morrison asks Lil, "Can you do me a favor?" "Sure boss what do you need?". "The School has refused to give me the list of students, maybe you can talk them into giving you the list I have been asking for?, I need the last two years, keep me in the loop. Right now I am going to get some shut eye."

Lil tapped Morrison on the shoulder, "Lieutenant wake up I have the information you are looking for", He rolled over smiling, "Sounds good what did you find?". "In the last two years there are four men on the roster I think we hit the jackpot?" Morrison, "Put their names and pictures up on the Game Board. We need to get their descriptions, where are they from, where are they now, what kind of students were they, what made them special to stand out from the rest of the class."

Lil started to describe to Morrison the male students. "Number One: James K, forty years old, six foot one inches tall, black hair, blue eyes, sounds like a ladies man, graduated top of his class, had a nice demeanor was mannerly to a fault. His teacher sensed that it was a cover for his true nature that all of his actions were rehearsed to hide his real personality."

"Number Two: Marty S, fair student from upstate Washington, kind of a mousey kid, twenty four years old, five foot ten inches, about one hundred and sixty pounds, graduated lower end of class, they think he went back home."

"Number Three: Henry J, small build about five feet five inches tall, weight one hundred seventy pounds, fair student, graduated middle of class, specialized in 3-D masks and make up, won school awards for portrayal of Hollywood Actors, location unknown, original home base unknown, was a loner, rumor was that he had a a personality clash with one of the female students.

"Number Four: Steve W, He was eighteen, home address LA, parents paid for his schooling, slight built, five foot eleven inches tall, brown hair, brown eyes, very shy, stayed mostly to himself was a hard worker, graduated lower end of his class last the school knew he was living with his parents.

Morrison thinks for a second and says to Lil, "I think we should look into number three Henry J, first, he more or less fits the Rapist profile, see if there is anymore info you can dig up on him, look up where he stayed while he was going to school, address, is he still in the LA area, maybe we can find his DNA and feed it into the FBI's data base, he could have left fingerprints."

Lil asks, "Maybe one of these characters has a criminal record. I'll check all four to see if they have ever been arrested." Morrison, "Sounds good to me, let me know what you find check this Henry guy out first, understand?" Lil, "Got you boss, he will be first on my list."

Morrison, "George don't waste your time I have all the information, thanks anyway."

The next morning Morrison drove to Norwalk, California it was the last address listed for the suspect on Maple street he had rented a one bedroom apartment moved out about six months ago. The chances of finding any DNA evidence or finger prints were nil to none, Morrison was a real bulldog once he planted his teeth into a case he wouldn't let go till he had all the answers. It took him two hours to drive to the address. "Damn LA traffic" he parked in front of the apartment walked to the front door rang the bell, there was momentary silence.

"Who is there?, I don't want anything, go away I'm sick." Morrison, "This is Lieutenant Morrison from the LA Police Department I talked to you yesterday concerning your tenant on the second floor his name was Henry J". "Oh Heavens! I remember please wait while I get the key we can enter from the side stairs. He has been gone for a few months." The door opened slowly and an old lady peeked out through a crack in the doorway.

She was wearing thick spectacles, dressed in what looked like an old flour sack. She asked Morrison, "Can I see your Identification please. You know in these times I have to be very careful there are hoodlums just looking to waylay an old lady."

CHAPTER: NINE

Morrison showed her his badge, "Have no fear Ma'am I am who I say I am could we please traverse to the apartment now? so I can inspect the apartment for evidence. OH, by the way sign this form allowing me to collect evidence without a warrant? the City will reimburse you for anything I decide is crucial to the case or any damages caused to the apartment." The Landlady answered, "Give it here sonny, just let me read it over before I sign. Have to be sure everything is on the up and up." She read the document, signed on the dotted line, without a word handed it back to Morrison turned motions for Morrison to follow slowly walked up the stairs to the apartment, was panting when she stopped at the top of the stairs and waited to catch her breath. Morrison wondered, "I hope to hell she doesn't have a HEART ATTACK." The Landlady out of breath proceeded to unlock the door and waived him in, "The place is a mess I haven't rented it since he left. He wasn't the cleanest renter I've ever had kept very strange hours. I know he was going to that Makeup School sometimes he wouldn't come in till early morning he always carried a strange looking bag with him. It kind of gave me the creeps, that is why I haven't rented the place since he left. Don't need the money or weird characters around."

Morrison looks around the flat asking, "If you don't mind I would like to look around by myself when I am done I will meet you at your place. There are a few questions you may be able to answer, like give me a description of your last tenant." "Yes, I will do that." After the Landlady left he stood in the apartment absorbing the silence glanced slowly around, went to the couch, turned on the lamp. Walked through the small dwelling lighting up every room, in the bedroom next to the bed on the wall could see the remnants of tape where the suspect had attached pictures. Next to the bed in a small trash can filled with shredded newspaper.

Morrison, "Well, well, What do we have here?" The first piece was the story of a unknown rapist who the local authorities had attributed to at least a dozen assaults on local women, they did not have any idea who he was, were helpless to stop his attacks on women.

Morrison read the headlines and just smiled, "I have that son of a bitch" he opened the dresser drawers and found women's undergarments he placed the matching bras and panties in separate evidence bags. Swabbed the sink, toilet, there were numerous hairs on the floor, finger prints. "This is a gold mine of evidence. This Henry was one sloppy bastard." Opening the closet in the bedroom there was a familiar smell. He took a deep breath it was a musky slaving lotion, he cogitated for a minute.

"I know why that scent is familiar, the last two attacks. It was enough to gag you the attacker had been wearing it, he has very poor taste." Placed what he had found in separate evidence bags, turned off the lights sealed the apartment with police tape, walked down the stairs and knocked on the Landlady's door, he still had a few questions he needed answers too. She opened the door, "Yes, young man what do you need to know?" Morrison questions the Landlady, "Can you tell me if Henry had any friends, did you ever see anyone ever pick him up? maybe people who visited him."

She answered, "Now that I think about it he did have someone pick him up a couple of times. The driver never left the car just sat there and honked the horn for Henry to come down. I would say about three or four times it wasn't long after that he moved out."

Morrison, "Could you give me a description of the driver was he young, old, the color of his hair, did he have an accent?" Land Lady, "He was driving a fairly new blue automobile two door, sounded like he may have been from back east, dark hair, well dressed maybe his age was late thirty's or early forties." Morrison stood there thinking, "Everything is falling into place. Her description of the visitor sounded like James K. Those two were friends probably accomplices in the rapes. There was something not quite right, something else was going on he could feel it. I have to check this James K's background."

He turns to the Landlady, "Did you happen to get a look at his license plate?". "Well now that you mention it one night I just happened to be looking out my window and said to myself write down his license plate number just in case I have to call the police if he he causes trouble." Morrison starts to laugh thinking.

"This old lady doesn't let anything get past her."

She pulled a crumpled piece of paper out of her pocket handing it to him, which he gladly accepted, "This could be the kicker. Thank you very much I have to leave now if you think of anything else please give me a call or leave a message. Here is my card with my cell number." He walked to his car very pleased with himself, "Hopefully I can wrap this up in short order. I will have one of them or both in the lockup shortly. Tomorrow I visit the school and see if I can gleam anymore information from the teachers or students, tonight I am getting myself a room so I can get a good nights sleep, I can start again tomorrow morning."When he arrived at the hotel he checked his GPS to see how far it was to the school from his room, estimated the drive was about a half an hour to the school. Took a shower, shaved, changed his clothes, spread the new evidence on the desk. Sat quietly turning the evidence bags over slowly trying to get into the perps minds. "Shit, shit enough I need a drink." He strapped on the holster, placed his gun, left the hotel room.

CHAPTER: TEN

orrison spots a liquor store parks his car, walks up to the clerk, "I'll take a fifth of the best bourbon on the shelf" the clerk places it on the counter. "That will be forty six and change." Morrison places a gift on the counter, "Keep the change." The clerk pulls out a paper bag wraps it around the bourbon. "Here you are sir have a nice night."

The door to the Liquor store opened with a loud bang.

Morrison saw the reflection of two men in the mirror directly behind the clerk, one of them had a sawed off shotgun, "SON OF A BITCH" Morrison thinks, he waves to the clerk, "get down behind the counter those two bulls are about to rob the store" The ugly looking thug raises the shotgun, hollers, "Hey, Mother Fucker I want everything in the register I want it now or you are both dead." Morrison had already unholstered his automatic and ducked behind a wine rack, "Just what I need a couple of druggies all high robbing a Liquor store. Tomorrow the stupid fucks probably won't remember where they are or what they did."

The big guy had a shaved head, with dragon tattoos crawling around his eye balls, long black scraggly beard, his pupils bugging out of his head like he wasn't all there before Morrison could calm them down he watched as Godzilla broke-open the shotgun jamming two shells into the gun and in one motion swung the shotgun around pulled the triggers on both barrels causing a mirror advertising Bourbon whiskey behind the counter to shatter into a million shards of glass.

He could hear the clerk hiding behind the counter scream, "OH MY GOD!!" as his body was showered with the glass needles and then silence, "JESUS," Morrison wondered if the poor bastard was still breathing. The second robber jumped over the counter and opened the cash register, "Hey brother there's a couple of hundred in the till". "Just put it in your pocket and if that stupid clerk is still breathing put a bullet in his head." Morrison crouched behind the wine racks thinking, "Did these assholes forget there was a customer in the store or are they getting ready to take me out?" out of the corner of his eye he caught glint of the robber behind the counter cock his automatic started to point it at the clerk. With out thinking he spun around fired twice both shots hit the shooter in the chest, he had a complete look of surprise dropping the weapon clutching his chest, blood oozing between his fingers there was a death rattle as he collapsed on the floor. Everything seemed to happen in slow motion the robber holding the sawed-off shot gun turned toward the counter looking as his partner collapsed. He broke open the sawed-off shot gun, reached into his coat pocket pulled out two shotgun shells started to insert them into the gun's chambers. Morrison jumped as the sound of the shotgun was being locked into place, the Hulk bellowed, "You are a dead man" and swung the gun in Morrison's direction to fire, just before he fired Morrison rolled behind a beer barrel. The blast totally destroyed the wine rack, scattering volumes of wine and shards of glass cascading against the wall. Before he could reload the shotgun Morrison fired from a kneeling position the bullet punctured his lower jaw blowing his brains out of the top of his head spreading them dripping from the ceiling, he stood straight up then fell back into the front door stone dead. "Jesus, what a mess I guess he can now be considered brain dead" Morrison started to laugh "GOD" what a frigging disaster. The local Police crashed through the Liquor Store doorway with guns drawn, "Everybody on the floor or we shoot, Smith check to see how many bodies there are" he looked at Morrison, "stand up while I cuff you." Morrison stood up staring at the Police Sergeant, "What in the hell are you looking at asshole I'll bust your frigging head?" Morrison smiled, "If you will look in my coat pocket you will find my badge Sergeant!, I just took these two morons out and saved the clerks life, so will you please remove the cuffs and I will follow you to the station and make a statement." The Clerk was a bit disheveled his face and clothes were stained with the robbers blood, he looked at the Police and spoke, "Look officers this man saved my life these two crazies crashed the store looking to rob and kill me, he shot both of them before they could, so he is a hero not a criminal."

"OK, OK, so he's a hero, Frank take off his cuffs you Morrison don't start any funny stuff". "I am not in the mood Sergeant lets get to the Station, so I can make my report and get to bed I haven't had any sleep in two days" Morrison quipped. "All right follow us and we'll get your statement so you can cut some zees", the Sergeant agreed.

Morrison walked into the motel at two thirty in the morning "Names Morrison my Department made a reservation for one day I'm a little late had a problem to take care of. OH, by the way can you book me for a second day I will have to stay in town longer than I figured?" Clerk, "Yea, we can accommodate you things are slow this time of the year, same room take the elevator on your left." Morrison wakes in the morning rolls over looking at the clock, "It's ten o'clock, Holy Shit, better get my butt moving." He does fifty pushups, twenty pull ups to warm up. Takes a hot shower, shaves, slips into a comfortable pair of slacks, puts on a shirt and a light summer jacket. Stands for a second thinking, "Should I take my Beretta?, yea, I would have a hard time explaining if someone should break into the room and the gun is missing." he straps on his holster and inserts the weapon. "It will make my day if I can collar those two."

CHAPTER: ELEVEN

He stops at the desk, "Are there any restaurants close by where I can get a good steak and a stiff drink?"

Clerk, "When you leave the hotel turn left one block down is the Squealing Pig Restaurant, good food, their not cheap on the booze." Morrison walks into the Restaurant and looks around, wondering what in the hell kind of place is this?, the Bartender notices him giving the place the glad eye. He hollers to Morrison, "Not to worry friend a lot of actors and students from the School hang out here. Some of them are made up just looking for a quick bite and a beer before they return to the set or their next class. Take a seat at the bar and relax."

Lieutenant Morrison is thinking, "If I keep my ears open I am sure someone here probably knows Henry or Jimmy. They may have been hanging in LA before school. What the hell no harm in asking can't loose anything." He leans over to the customer closest to him asking, "Do you know a couple of guys their names are Henry J. and Jimmy K.?, I am new in town we hung around together. I think they went to the Art School for makeup just down the street. Would appreciate any info so I could reconnect." The customer looks Morrison up and down, Morrison is ready for the guy to start a fight, "Names Jake, tell you what buy me a drink I know where they used to room, but that was quite a while ago. Word on the street is someone wants to put a hurt on the both of them. You wouldn't be wanting or looking to do that would you?". "Hell no, I'm just in from back east wanted to meet up with them and see what they had going on. No sweat man I'll find them on my own." Jake answers, "Look man, I didn't mean to insult you just being careful. You never know for sure who you are talking to you could be a cop or one of the Enforcers looking for them so you have to be careful."

Morrison thinks, "This place could be gold mine of information, there seems to be a hell of a lot going on under the table around here. I'll buy this guy a few drinks to loosen him up and maybe he will spill the beans about what is happening below the surface." Morrison, "HEY BAR KEEP, how about another drink?", he motioned to the Bartender, "Set Jake up with another," "OK Chief." He sets a shot glass upside down in front of Jake, "Thanks man what did you say your name was?". "Names Frank, I don't have anything else to do tonight, so let's party it's on me."

Jake shakes his head, "OK, But just one more, I have a gig tonight at Midnight and I have to be sober or my ass will be in a sling. If your around tomorrow night we can put on a real drunk. I'll be free after tonight for a couple of days."

When Jake leaves Morrison notices that at the back of the Restaurant there are numerous women's garments and mens clothes hanging from hooks on the far wall. Morrison asks the Bartender, "What's with clothes hanging from the wall somebody have a fetish?", Bartender smiles answering, "No on weekends after hours there is a contest to see what women can dress like men,the men dress like women, the fee is five hundred dollars per. There are prizes for the winners and everyone gets hammered and we ORGY till everyone drops. You know men on men, women on women and maybe threesomes, etc, etc."

Morrison ponders his reply, "Sounds cool if I had five large maybe I'd enter but right now I have an appointment." He leaves the bar and drives back to Henry's old apartment, knocks on the Landlady's door. She answers, "Lieutenant what can I do for you?". "If you don't mind I would like to inspect Henry's apartment again if that's Ok, with you". "No problem here's the key, just bring it back when you'r done." He entered the apartment, removed a half a dozen hooks from the wall carefully placed them in separate evidence bags. He took out his fingerprint kit checking every inch of the apartment with a fine tooth comb. Found a print on the flush lever of the commode a second print on the inside of the medicine cabinet.

Someone had wiped down the rest of the apartment with bleach household cleaner. The apartment reeked of a strong detergent odor, this guy was no dummy but he was pissing me off he was like a wisp in the wind. Everywhere they go I am given a different description, "When I called the School this morning both Henry and Jimmy never showed up for their class pictures or diplomas" Morrison is thinking, "This pair is into something else besides molesting women. It's almost as if they do it for entertainment."

Morrison left the apartment returned the key, placed the evidence in a sealed container sent it overnight to the State forensics lab to check for DNA. He returned to the hotel wanting to relax for a couple of hours before bar hopping.

The elevator door opened and he had a strange feeling like he was being watched. He reached for his Beretta slipping it silently from the holster, holding it close to his side. When he reached his room the door was open a crack, pushed the door open gun in hand, looking around the room was empty he could see someone had been rifling through his belongings. Walking to the bureau drawer saw that the silk thread that he had wrapped around the pull was broken, opened the it the evidence was missing. "I wonder what in the hell they were looking for?" he thought back to when he had entered the hotel the girl behind the counter had picked up the phone. She was warning someone that I was on the way up to my room. I don't know what I'm into there is more going on here than my chasing a serial rapist." He checked out of the hotel in the morning drove to the main Police Station in the city of Los Angeles. He approached the desk and identified himself asked if he could meet with the Detective that handles sexual assaults.

The Sergeant said, "Let me check to see if she is at her desk" he dialed her number, Morrison could hear the phone ringing, "Hello, Detective Macia". "There is a Lieutenant Morrison here that would like to talk to you". "What does he want?". "He is trying to find a serial rapist and would like to coordinate his findings with the LA Police Department". "GOOD, sent him up!" "Take the elevator to the sixth floor turn right her name is Detective Macia she's waiting for you." Morrison exited the elevator stopped at her desk extending his hand introduced himself, "Detective Macia my name is Lieutenant Morrison I am trying to track down a suspected Rapist his name is Henry J. he may have a partner whose name is Jimmy K. I think they are into more than assaulting women, from what I can gleam someone has put out a hit on them." Laura looks Morrison up and down before answering, "You have been a busy boy for the last couple of days, yes I am aware of both of them. The word on the street is they robbed someone in the Russian Mafia then tried to screw over whoever set it up"."NO Shit! Do you have a description of these two?". "Jimmy K. has a record Henry no, there is no positive description for Henry." She reached into her desk drawer and laid a dossier on the desk top. "I will have a copy made for you, yes we have had a rash of assaults that I haven't been able to solve. The perp seems to be a chameleon. Every time I process a victim or a witness they give me a different description", Morrison answers, "These two are graduates of the Makeup School here in LA and are experts at manufacturing real life masks. I will keep you up to on what I learn." Morrison, "I will be here for at least another week tracking down leads I'll follow those two to the ends of the earth."

CHAPTER: TWELVE

*J*ack Morrison rolled out of bed, it was three in the morning he dialed his bosses number. The phone rang three times, Jack just let it ring again and again, he heard someone on the other end pick up, "WHO IN THE HELL IS THIS…!" Jack smiling on the other end, "Hi boss Jack Morrison here I need at least another week here maybe a little longer this has turned into a much larger case than I thought" he stopped talking holding the phone at arms length, "YES, YES take all the time you need just don't screw up" the Chief hung up mumbling, "that damned Morrison drives me nuts."

Jack smiling, "The only way to get what you want with him is get him out of bed at three and he will give in just to go back to sleep." Morrison was having his morning coffee, when his cell phone rang. "Hello who is this?". "Frank Jacobs from downtown Detective Macia wants me to work with you on this case I would like to meet with you to review whatever information you have." "OK, where do you want to meet?". "How about the Main Police Station downtown at say noon". "Sounds good, I'll bring everything I have, see you at twelve." At noon Lieutenant Morrison signed in showing his badge, "What floor is Detective Jacobs located on?". "Do you have an appointment?". "At noon". "Take the elevator on the left he's on the fifth floor."

He walks over to Jacobs desk and announces his presence and lays the file on the desktop. "This is everything I have so far." "Happy to meet you Jack I think we can work well together."

"We have had a half a dozen attacks in the last couple of months. The victims are so badly beaten they are unable to give us a description. The attacker is tall, or short, or blonde, heavy, thin. It's driving us nuts the only thing we have found is silicone under one of the victims fingernails." Jack's ears perk up, "That's what I have so far I believe that there may be two of them working together". "They both went to the School in Hollywood were trained to make 3-D real life masks on the computer. That makes sense we have had a couple of burglaries in the Beverly Park neighborhood. The thieves knew all the alarm codes, where the safe was, the combination. They occurred right around when the attacks occurred". "So your take is that somehow the attacks and robberies are connected". "It seems to be a coincidence but then I don't believe in coincidences. The only tie to the robberies is a high class call girl Marjorie Swift who was having affairs with both of the owners. Apparently she is a real partier and will do anything including drugs."

Jack, "Did she have an alibi?" Frank, "She had solid alibis for both robberies. There were a dozen witnesses who swore she never left their sight. So we had to let her go." Frank, "There definitely seems to be a thread that connects her to our two felons and the attackers. I think we should call her back and question her again. Tell her we have pictures of the people we think committed the robberies and we would like her to see if she can identify them." Frank, "We could try she wasn't very cooperative the last time. Knowing her she would want three hundred an hour just to talk to us", he says laughing.

Jack, "WOW, this town is full of Prima Donnas, apparently everyone thinks their shit doesn't stink, I guess your used to it now." "I have a question for you the women seemed to be attacked at random. How did your victims become involved with the mugger." Frank, "They all met their attacker on the Internet he uses the code name Henry sets up a time and place where they will meet at the meeting he attacks them knocks the hell out of them and has sex. Strips them nude and ties them up. We have been lucky so far that no-one has been killed. "Jack," That is the same "MO" he used up state. The son of a bitch has a big pair of balls used the same name. I knew I was onto something big, there is the smell of something much bigger going on. Somehow everything is connected." Frank, "I'll call this Marjorie Swift invite her to visit us." Jacobs picked up the phone and dialed her number, it rang three times went to voice mail. He looked at Morrison and shook his head. Jack Morrison, "Why don't you just leave her a message tell her to meet us at the police station at two or we will come to your apartment bring you in handcuffs. See if that gets a raise out of her." Jack, "You know she won't answer the phone or come to the Police Station don't you?, we have to stir the pot see what happens. I don't think we will get very much from our little Marjorie."

"By the way what are you doing later?". "I'm going to the Squealing Pig for a few drinks. If you are up to it I'll see you there at eight and be prepared this place is a hoot. There are some weird dudes that hang out at that place."

Frank, "I know the place see you there at eight." Jack Morrison started the rental car and thought, "What do I want for dinner?, I need a good thick steak I can charge it on my expense account haven't had a good meal since I arrived." He turned down the street and drove to Carletios Steak House, pulled into the parking lot and turned off the car.

Walked into the Restaurant and sat at the bar. "What would you like to drink sir?, we have a great variety of beer on tap, good wine list, any mixed drink."

"I'll have a double Bourbon on the rocks make me the biggest steak in the house burned on both sides and rare in the middle, baked potato with all the trimmings and a salad." After the meal Jack sat back and relaxed ordering another drink he looked over the customers in the restaurant. He noticed a couple in the back booth they were also customers at the Squealing Pig the other night. He leans over the bar asks the bartender, "Have you ever heard of the Squealing Pig?". "Yea, why do you ask I go there all the time I belong to the Private Club. We meet a couple of times a month." Jack, "Just wondered I was there a couple of days ago. It seemed to be a real jumping place, lots of friendly folks." Bartender, "You a cop or something?". "No, No! Just looking for a place to have a few drinks and relax." He finished his drink, thinking, "It's almost eight I better go Jacobs will be at the bar waiting." Jake was sitting at the bar when Frank entered. "Come join us, we were talking about the Private Club they are having a show tonight at midnight, even non-members can dress up and perform." Frank started to laugh, "Hell yes I can play a guitar." Jacobs, "We can sing." Bartender, "Fee is Fifty Dollars per person". "We're in what do you say Jake, let's have a go." Jake, "Frank you are one crazy ass, I say we party."

CHAPTER: THIRTEEN

arjorie calls her lawyer, "Hey Morty that cop called me wants me to come to the Police Station so they can question me again about the robberies. Do I have to or can I just ignore him?" Morty, "Just ignore him if he calls again tell him you are too busy. If he has questions tell him to put it in writing you will have your lawyer send a reply. By the way I set you up with a customer his wife is on vacation in Europe, just make sure I get my cut when you are through, I hope you understand?" Marjorie, "Keep your cool Morty you know I never skim". "What about the last heist, where are the jewels, cash. The people I work for are not happy. You screw up again they will find you wearing cement shoes" Morty quips. She screams, "I told you those two assholes wounded one of my crew. Hell, there was a shoot out in broad daylight. It could have blown our entire operation. I have been trying to track them down so far no luck I have a few people looking for them, they must have skipped town." Morty, "Forget it, The mark hangs out at the Yacht Club. I've set it up so you will be a guest at the club ask for Robbie he knows the drill the mark is there every night his name is Carl he puts the make on any female that is single. You won't have any trouble just go back to his place scope it out then get back to me, understand?". "I hear you

Morty, I hear you. No problem." Marjorie stands in front of the mirror wondering, "What in the hell did I get my self into two years ago I was an Undercover Black Op then everything went South. The operation went all to hell my people were ambushed I had to go rogue. The CIA blamed me and claimed I was a Double Agent and had to be taken out." She went underground was selling her ass setting up marks, to make enough money to keep her daughter in a Private School. She had faked her own death as far as she could tell the CIA had bought it. Marjorie slips into a tight dress spinning around admires her still firm body, still good looks. She was five foot eight inches, blond hair, blue eyes, a hard body. "You still have it baby, screw Morty those jewels pay for my daughters next semester in School and allows me to keep Susan Alcott as my daughters Guardian. I think this will be my last scam."

She enters the garage and climbs into her Mercedes Benz S65 Coupe, that will turn heads no one will question why she is at the club. They are Snobs, that is why I love to screw over them most of the time they are embarrassed to call the cops or even admit they have been taken. When the Valet parks her car she asks for Robbie. The Valet calls to the Door Man, "Hey Mike tell Robbie that Marjorie is here" Door man, "Your guest has arrived."

"I will escort her in." Robbie gives Marjorie a hug and ushers her into the club, he points out her mark, "He's there at the back table slobbering over those two women. Do them a favor and when you get his attention let him take you to his place so you can scope it out." She sat at the bar and pulled her skirt up over her knee rocked back and forth giving him a "come over" smile every time he looked up. Marjorie nodded her head calling Carl to come over and talk.

It took about ten minutes, he was sitting next to her, "Can I buy you a drink?, damn woman I could leave home for someone with your looks. Maybe even divorce my wife except she has more money than I do." He laughs asking "What's your name?". "Marjorie, what's yours?". "Just call me Carl why don't I take you to my estate we can party?". "Sounds good to me I'll follow in my own car." She thinks, "this should be a piece of cake this slob is falling down drunk." "Give me your address I will meet you at your place in about thirty minutes I have my own car, I don't want to leave it at the Club overnight." She watched as he left waited for the Valet to bring her car to the front of the Club, as she entered her Mercedes tipped him twenty, thinking, "What the hell he has to work for a living." Marjorie stopped at the gated Mansion, just siting there for a couple minutes, "Wow how did some people get so filthy rich? this place must be worth millions." Morty sure knew how to pick them. "This place must be a gold mine all I have to do is play it normal get pictures, give a little sex, slip the slob a couple of sleeping pills get him to blab about his money, safe combination then be on her way to a nice haul." She punched the code into the gate monitor as it opened slowly drove her Mercedes up the circular driveway. The mansion had to be at least twenty thousand square feet it was a French Chateau straight out of France. Parked her car in front of the house walked up the steps looking at the opulence and details of the home. Stopped at the massive entrance doors ornately decorated with with a filigree of gold, before she could reach for the handle the doors swung silently open.

CHAPTER: FOURTEEN

"Come in, Come in I have been waiting for you. The servants have the night off so we have the night to ourselves, follow me to my Play Room." He waved his hand the doors closed as silently as they opened. She followed him to into the elevator it stopped at the lower level, when the doors opened there was a space that would hold at least one hundred people, there were lush couches, chairs strewn around the space, screens on the walls, cameras, a bar to the left that would dwarf most establishments and last but not least on the far wall were whips, chains,she recognized a body bag. Carl slowly turned facing Marjorie in his hand was a lead sap, "You bitch, have screwed over me for the last time. Those jewels belong to me. Morty set your dumb ass up, they will find your body parts all over LA. I will have the pleasure of killing you slowly." Striding across the floor swinging the sap. She acted without thinking ducked when he attempted to cave in the back of her head. She was back in the Black Ops, thinking, "Thank God I keep in shape practicing self defense." Marjorie rolled to the floor came up into a crouched position about fifteen feet in front of Carl, she pulled a knife from her boot threw it at his menacing form as he advanced toward her. He all of a sudden was stone cold he had been acting inebriated. "These bastards set me up they are all part of the mob." The knife penetrated his left shoulder he stopped in bewilderment and screamed in pain, "YOU FRIGGING BITCH! I WILL RIP YOUR HEAD OFF, after I screw you every way, but loose, who do you think you are screwing with me? Robbie is one of my people we set you up to go down as an example hard, real hard. You thought you could mess with me. I will make you wish you weren't born." As he was screaming his tirade the blood was spurting from the knife wound. Reaching over with his right hand pulled the knife from his left arm, that was a mistake the blood flowed faster. He felt his legs buckling under him as he collapsed on the floor in a coma.

Marjorie, "Shit, with his blood loss he will be dead in a couple of minutes." She stood watching as he was bleeding to death, "Jesus Christ, what a screwed up scenario, I have an ugly fat asshole dying on the floor. The cops will never believe I acted in self defense, they have been trying to tag me for those robberies and here I stand about to be accused of murder."

Marjorie went over to Carl laying on the floor he was white she could see the life draining out of him. She rolled him over grabbed a towel that was laying on the couch wrapped it around his damaged arm,turned the tourniquet as tight as she could. The flow of blood slowed to a trickle. "Now what?" she just couldn't leave him lying there. She pulled out her cell phone no signal. Looked around trying to find a house phone, spotted one on the bar picked it up "thank God there's a signal." Marjorie dialed Morty, picked up on the first ring, "Is it all done Carl?". "You son of a bitch Morty you set me up he's on the floor bleeding to death. Get an ambulance here now I will be long gone", she looks around wondering, "I would like to know what other secrets he has hidden down here?" Morty, "Marjorie just stay there I have a couple of my boys on the way over as we speak. Leave the front door open I gave them the code for the gate so they can enter without any problems. Should be there in fifteen minutes, trust me sweetheart I will take care of everything, trust me!!" Marjorie, "Fuck you you god damed weasel" slammed the phone. Marjorie didn't like the whole setup these bastards were trying to kill me. She started wiping down anything she had touched, washed the knife in the bathroom then poured a half gallon of bleach to mask the blood.

"Morty's boys can clean up the rest of this mess. I am out of here I have a feeling there are bodies buried all over this lower level." Following her instincts she runs out of the house starts her car and leaves rubber as she exits the Estate, thinking. "I need a place to stay low for awhile." Nick and Two Fingers drive in five minutes after Marjorie leaves. The gate was open so they just pulled up to the front of the house. "Nick grab the rags, bleach from the back of the car, we can come back for the body bag later, anything else we might need." Two Fingers, "I will take care of the broad she knows too much to live, if you know what I mean. We need to get moving or Morty will be on our asses." They enter the house looking for Marjorie, no one is around the place is as silent as a tomb. "Let's take the elevator down we have to start cleaning up. We have to be out of here before the sun comes up." Nick, "Just don't touch anything with out gloves on, we have to leave this place cleaner than when we found it". "I don't need any Mick telling me what to do."

They walk out of the elevator and hear someone moaning. "Holy Shit, Carl is still breathing. Call Morty and find out what he wants us to do with the body". "Morty this is Two Fingers, Carl is still breathing the broad must have split as soon as she hung up, what do we do now boss? Take him out or call an Ambulance he has a tourniquet on his arm."

Morty, "No don't call an Ambulance to the house see if you can get him in the back of the SUV drop him off at the Hospital. We don't need the Cops nosing around the house there are some things such as the whips, chains and other things that may make them suspicious, dig deeper into what really goes on at the mansion." They clean up the blood and check to see if anything else is out of place, "Go to the SUV bring me the Fluorescein Spray I want to check the rugs, furniture for blood splatters. Any furniture or rugs that have blood stains we remove burn." Nick and Two fingers carry Carl to the SUV drop him off at the Emergency Room. They return to the house remove the couch, chair all the area rugs, "There is a dump an hour drive from here we will dump it there and burn it."Two Fingers,"this shit is driving me nuts I don't clean my own house here I am playing housekeeper. If we're lucky the Police won't connect the house to Carl's stabbing. We can return in the morning to make sure we haven't missed anything."

CHAPTER: FIFTEEN

Marjorie didn't return to her apartment she stayed at a hotel on the other end of town. She dyed her hair dark brown, trashed the cell phone, bought two burners, next morning went to her bank cleaned out her checking account and her safety deposit box, burned her credit cards. Checked the Canadian Passport that was in her safety box making sure it was up to date, bought a bus ticket to Edmonton,Canada disappeared into the backcountry. "I know that son of a bitch set me up. They were getting revenge for me skimming a few jewels, ten thousand dollars. I hope this doesn't alert the CIA to the fact that I'm still breathing. I probably would have been tortured and killed, screw those bastards and the horses they rode in on luckily I kept my cabin in the woods."

Morrison, "have you received a response from our lady of the night?, it's been over a week. We may as well pick her up at the bar she owns on the South side of town. We'll take a ride after lunch put the squeeze on her, would love to hear her squeal like the little pig she is." "Sounds good to me, we have to get off center this case is dragging on and on. My case files are piling up on my desk as we speak." They go down to the nearest Deli for a corned beef and a beer. Then drive to the South side to visit Marjorie's place, Morrison thinks, "I will never get used to the sprawl, congestion in Los Angeles thank God for the suburbs." Jack pulls up to the curb the bar appears to be closed. He exits the car and reads a note on the door, "Under New Management" will open 8:00 pm tonight.

He hollers to Morrison in the car, "It looks like she has skipped town. We need to come back at eight tonight to talk to the new owner." Morrison, "I say we put out an APB on the bitch, we have to check all forms of transportation out of town. I agree we'll come back tonight to see if the new owner has any clue as to where in the hell she went." Back at the Precinct Jack, "I've checked the Cab Company, Train Station and Airlines they don't have any one leaving LA that fits her description. Her Mercedes has been spotted parked in a lot downtown no Marjorie to be found, I told the Parking Attendant to give us a call if she shows up or someone moves the car", "OK, we've done all we can now lets drive over to the South side and question the new owner." They arrived at the Bar a little after eight the parking lot was full, "Damn this place is Rocking." When they entered the Bar customers were five deep at the bar ordering drinks. Jack elbowed his way to the front showing his Badge, "I need to see the owner", the bartender pointed to a table at the back, "The bald guy dressed in a red shirt". "OK, thanks." He waved to Morrison and they both approached the table and sat down. "Are you the new owner?". "Yea what do you want" Jack, "We are looking for Marjorie Swift, I thought she owned this place."

Owner, "I got a phone call last night she made me an offer I couldn't refuse. She offered me the place at half price if I could seal the deal before midnight with cash. I've been trying to buy her out for a couple of years couldn't pass it up." Jack, "Do you have any idea where she went?" Owner, "Not a clue she signed over the deed was gone. I thought it was a little strange, if you know Marjorie she is a little loopy." Jack, "Frank I think we should check out her Mercedes." Frank's cell phone rang, "Hello Captain what up?", the Captain gave him an address in Hollywood, "The neighbors are complaining that the Mansion next door is being robbed", "Yes sir we will be there in thirty minutes."

"Lets go Jack a Mansion in Hollywood is being ransacked." They headed for the location of the robbery. When they arrived there was a Police Car blocking the entrance. They had to park on the road and walk up the driveway to the Mansion. Morrison, "Who own's this place? It must be worth millions. I wonder what is going on there must be half of the Precinct here. Lets go in and check it out." Frank, "Sergeant were from downtown this is Lieutenant Jack Morrison, I'm Detective Jacobs any evidence of a break-in, is anything missing?". "No, as a matter a fact we can't find anything out of place. The neighbors said there was activity in and out of the place all night by sunrise the house was as silent as a tomb. The neighbors did get the license plates of two automobiles, one was a Rolls Royce the other a Mercedes they were gone before we arrived." Jacobs, "Give me the plate numbers I will track down the owners." He went to the car entered the plate numbers into the computer data base. He just whistled as the owners were identified. The Mercedes owner was Marjorie Swift and the Rolls Royce was Carl Karlissone the owner of the Mansion. Jacobs just sat looking at the computer readout.

"What in the hell is going on? Just for the Hell of it I'm going to check if any patients have been signed in the Hospital Emergency Rooms in the last twenty four hours with gun shot or stab wounds."

The Computer showed a patient with stab wounds whose name is Carl Karkissone in critical condition. He calls to Jack, "Come on down to the car we have to go to the Hospital the Mercedes belonged to our missing Miss Marjorie Swift, the Rolls Royce to Carl the owner of the Mansion, who by the way is in on life support with stab wounds." Detective Frank Jacobs calls the Sergeant, "Sergeant I would like you to remove all our personnel from the Mansion and put a guard on the front door. It appears that the house is the scene of an attempted murder. I am going to the hospital to question Carl the owner. Have a forensic team at the house by noon." The two Officers drove to the hospital. Frank "Now we know why Marjorie disappeared it appears she tried to kill Carl or at the least she is somehow involved." When they arrived at the hospital Jack questioned the nurse on duty, "Do you have a patient registered whose name is Carl who was the victim of a knife attack", "Yes, he's in surgery and it will be at least three days before he will be able to identify his attacker."

CHAPTER: SIXTEEN

They drove back to the Mansion as Frank parked the Police Car his phone rang, "Hello, who is this?". "This is Carl's lawyer my name is Sam Morty what do you mean by attempting to question my client without his legal consul being present."

Frank, "Your client is in the hospital because he was stabbed almost bled to death."

Morty, "You are mistaken, I caution that the Police do not question my client about his injury without consul present. There is no proof of any attack if you do the city of Los Angelis will be sued, good by!". there was a loud clang as he hung up.

Frank just looked at Jack, "I wonder what that's all about, I say we check the house from top to bottom they are hiding something". "Sounds good by me brother lets rip that Mansion a new asshole." When they pulled up to the front entrance Lieutenant Morrison sat there thinking, "we are missing something, Frank this house must have a lower level, play room they don't mess up the main house. Did the team find anything?" Frank, "They didn't find any lower level just the three upper floors, no sign of anything being disturbed."

He walked slowly around the first floor feeling the wall.

When he passed a clothes closet, stopped went back opened the closet door walked inside. The closets configuration mimicked the shape of a small elevator. Feeling along the interior wall found a loose panel pushed a button it slid open revealing the elevator controls.

"I'll be the son of a bee, I knew there was a lower level. Let's go bud we are going for a ride." The elevator stopped the doors slid open. In front of them was a very large game room that only the wealthy could afford. They walked slowly out into the space on the far wall was the faint outline where whips and chains had hung had been removed, now were barely visible their forms had been burned into the wall by the bright lights.

Jack, "What do we have here?, Look for a rear entrance to the lower level, they sure as hell couldn't have moved all this furniture bar down this elevator it's too small."

He walked to the back wall pulled back the black curtains revealing two large doors that opened to a freight elevator. The upper entrance was disguised with false grass.

Jack, "Hey Sarge bring the Forensic Crew around the back of the building there's a freight elevator that will hold all your equipment." When the entire team was in place he lowered the elevator the team went to work. "Ok, people time to go to work I will bet my life that this is the place where the confrontation took place, as to why is anyone's guess. Check all the furniture, rugs the bar for blood spatters, prints." Jack walked around looking for any furniture or rugs that had been replaced. The rug around the bar appears to have been replaced the furniture had that new smell. It appeared someone had cleaned the lower level to conceal any evidence of a crime with luck they had missed something. The Team at first could not find any trace of blood or finger prints. Jack, "Pull up all the rugs spray the concrete slab with Fluorescein Spray." The Team sprayed the bare concrete and specs of blood appeared all around the bar. A number of finger prints were on the phone.

"Alright, alright we now have a crime scene, take pictures of every inch of this level. I'll see how this floats with the Captain. I'm sure our friend Morty has talked to the Police Commissioner who has called the Precinct Captain. I wouldn't be surprised if this goes nowhere we sure tried."

Cell phone service was not possible in the Lower Level of the house when they reached the upper floor their phones started to ring. Even Morrisons phone as was the Forensic Teams. Frank answered first, "This is Captain Schmidt get your asses down here now and make sure you bring the entire team including our visiting Lieutenant Morrison and what ever evidence you think you have. I have been trying to get in touch with you for over an hour." Frank smiled, "I think the Captain is pissed, he just slam dunked the phone I'll bet it broke." They both started to laugh thinking they were in hot water. When they pulled up to the Station the Captain was waiting on the steps, waving everyone inside. He growled, "Get everyone into the conference room NOW, take all the evidence with you, what in the hell took you so long?". "The lower level of the Mansion was sound proof. We didn't have any communication with the outside. The team found blood splatters, finger prints there definitely was stabbing" the Captain's face turns red, "I have had calls from the Commissioner, the Mayor some Lawyer named Morty telling me to back off because there has been no proof of a crime committed, plus he tells me you two were told to stop or he would sue the pants off of the city. If one word of this leaks out about what went down today I will personally have your heads, if you think I'm kidding I'm not you will all be walking a beat". "Yes sir Captain, mum is the word. You have all the evidence it's in the conference room I'm not about to lose my job over a stabbing". "Don't be a wise ass Frank, go get a drink this never happened." Frank, "Hey Jack let us get out of here and get a drink." Jack, "Sounds good to me, the Pub downtown would be great." As they were driving downtown to get a drink the pair were staring out the windshield of the Police Car they both started laughing in unison. They laughed so hard tears ran down their faces. "The Captain was so frigging mad I thought he would blow a gasket. He knows damn well there was a stabbing until this Carl wakes up his hands are tied. Our lady of the night had something to sell but what she was selling this guy wasn't buy-ing he wanted more for his money than she was willing to give." Jack, "Just think of those whips and chains hanging on his wall. I say we get shit faced and pick up a couple of babes, what do you say?" Frank, "I'm in for a good toot. I have a wife and three kids at home, no women." "OK by me, with our luck we would be arrested by the Vice Squad." Jack woke up the next morning with one hell of a hangover. Crawling out of bed went to the fridge pulled a bottle of tomato juice mixed it with a beer that always seemed to ease his hangover. Thinking, "I need something to eat", got dressed walked to the Diner across the street and sat at the counter and ordered, "I'll have three eggs over easy, double toast, rasher of bacon and coffee, Oh and don't forget the hash browns." Jack sat there eating listening to the news on the television in the background caught his attention, "A five million dollar Mansion in Hollywood burned to the ground the Fire Marshal saying it appears to be arson", he turned to look at the television there was a picture of the Chateau before the fire and a second picture of the Chateau in ashes. "What the hell is going on, there is definitely something they are trying to hide now the Captain won't be able to stop the investigation." Carl was out of the Coma, "Well did you find out where the Bitch disappeared to?, your idea of teaching her a lesson back-fired", Morty, "She may talk or not I have no idea where she went to ground. We will have to revamp our entire operation most of our contacts in the city are running scared. The Captain is about to have a heart attack and all the Political flunkies won't even answer their phones till the Carl, "I say we lay low for a couple of months till the dust settles. It will cost us quite a few dollars but we don't need trouble so far we have stayed under the radar."

Morty, "I will keep looking for her if she's hiding on the West Coast I'll find her make no mistake."

CHAPTER: SEVENTEEN

After the score in Cleveland Jimmy and Henry drove west headed to Chicago hoping the Police in Ohio would have a heck of a time tying them to the last scam. Jimmy, "I have a score set up in Chicago's River North Neighborhood. I called one of my squeezes who works at the local Country Club she has set us up with a Temporary Members Pass. He had been able to contact three likely clients who were in the million dollar bracket," Jimmy thinking, "The use of the Club would give me the cover I need to make the Clients think I was in their league." As soon as they were settled in their room Jimmy did his routine of making calls to set up a meeting with a mark. His second call picked up, "Hello Clara, this is Jimmy we spoke about your investing in the market a week ago. I hope you have been watching the market the stock we spoke of went up ten percent in just one week." Clara, "That sounds fantastic,I am sold can we connect this week", "Why yes, Why don't we have lunch at the North Country Club tomorrow say at noon. I will have my chauffeur pick you up at eleven and drive you to the Club and we can relax and have a few drinks." Clara, "Very good I will see you tomorrow at twelve."

Jimmy hung up the phone, "Harry, lets go, you are going to need a monkey suit. I have a mark set up for tomorrow I told her my chauffeur will pick her up at eleven tomorrow and drive her to the club by noon. She lives on the upper North Side her name is Miss Clara she is a widow her husband left her a wealthy woman. Probably our sting could get us a half a million big ones." Henry, "Then what we need is to lay low for a while I am sure the cops will be hot on our asses." Jimmy, "I say we go South maybe Florida, what do you say we could both use a little sun." Henry, "Sounds like a plan brother, sounds like a plan." Henry could care less he needed a release, "I have to open my computer set up a date with a bleeding heart while we are in the Chicago area. I need a few souvenirs to hang on my wall." Jimmy, "There's a place a couple of blocks away that rents tuxes. I have your specs I'll pay for a quick fix on the tux be back in the hour." There was a knock on the door, "Henry let me in I have the Suit open the door." Jimmy, "Henry try the suit on, it will do the trick she will think I'm a high roller especially with my own man, what do you think?" Henry, "Jimmy I must admit you are a real con man. If I didn't know better I would believe that you are who you claim you are". "Let's get rolling we have to pick up the Rental Limousine after we pick it up you pick up Miss Clara and I will drive straight to the Club so I will be there waiting for her arrival." The Limo dropped her off at exactly twelve noon. He was waiting for her with her favorite drink a Mint Julep. "OH My! You are a dear I hope it has double bourbon." "Why yes Miss Clara I strive to please, sit down I have ordered lunch for the both of us." She was ecstatic things were looking up this would be an easy score the old bag had oodles of money he would take her for an easy half a million.

"Well Miss Clara after we have a light lunch we can proceed to your place, close the deal. How about another drink". "Of course another Mint Julep will be fine." When the waiter walked to the table, Jimmy whispers, "Make sure to put a little more juice in the next one she likes the drinks strong. I'll make sure you are taken care of." They sat and drank for about an hour making small talk after three more drinks Jimmy didn't want her drunk. She had papers to sign giving him authority to raid her bank accounts. He called Henry, "Bring the Limo around in twenty minutes I have her where I want her. In order to close the deal she has to give me power of Attorney. My make believe lawyer delivered the papers to her house." The forged papers appeared to be from a legit Brokerage Firm as soon as she signed them her money would disappear into an Overseas Bank never to be seen again. Jimmy thinking, "Maybe we should head to the islands instead of Florida." Morrisons cell phone rings, "Hello, who is this?". "Sergeant Michaels in Cleveland I have an elderly couple who have been scammed and the description of the two people who robbed them matches your Bolo. The pair also used their names Jimmy and Henry, this Jimmy seems to be main character he would set up the marks Henry would be his backup enforcer". "Have you been able to locate them?". "We think they are headed to Chicago, you are the expert on their mode of operation. If you can break away all your expenses will be picked up your help would be greatly appreciated."

CHAPTER: EIGHTEEN

"Well, Miss Clara how have you enjoyed your afternoon so far?". "Have been having the time of my life. I will definitely invest in your company you seem a very honest likable young man." Henry was waiting for a call from Jimmy when his cell phone rings Henry, "Ah Chauffeur please bring the car around Miss Clara will be leaving shortly." Jimmy did a slight of hand dropped a small amount of scopolamine (Devils Breath) in her drink. "Here Miss Clara you still have some Mint Julep left why don't we drink up so we can return to your house and complete your Investment Portfolio. I am sure you will be pleased with the return on Investment." He sat there waiting for her to finish the drink. The Devils Breath normally effected the victim almost immediately. They would do anything they were ordered to do and after it wore off the victim did not remember what had transpired. She finally tipped the glass swallowed the last vestige of her Mint Julep. Miss Clara sat there glassy eyed not moving. Jimmy thinking,"I have a few hours to complete the transaction and have her sign over her rights to half of her estate. The money would disappear into his over seas bank account in the Islands. Any evidence that he or Henry ever existed would disappear with the money". "Well Miss Clara the Limo has arrived, why don't you stand up and wave goodbye to all the good folks in the club and walk with me to the Limo." Doing as she was ordered left the Club walked slowly to the Limo. Henry held the door open so she could enter the Limo sitting down. Henry looked at Jimmy, "What's with her she seems to be in a trance". "She is in a trance, I slipped her some juice that will make her do anything I want for at least two hours. So step on it I am going to screw her out of as much of her money as possible." Henry drove as fast as he dared he didn't want the Police to stop him for speeding, getting a ticket. When they arrived at the house he pushed the button to open the garage door and drove right into the belly of the Mansion. Henry, "OK, we're here now what?" Jimmy, "Let's get her upstairs and have her open the safe, we get her bank codes and transfer a few million to my bank in the Islands, by the time she comes around we will be long gone taking a long vacation. Till I can set up another sucker we can drain." They helped Miss Clara to the elevator and the trio exited on the second level. Jimmy stopped for a few seconds and glanced around looking for the office. "There it is take a left". "Where is your safe I need your bank codes so we can open it to complete our transaction, is it alarmed? please write the information on this pad so there won't be any problems." After she had written the necessary information she handed it to Jimmy, "Miss Clara please sit here while we open the safe I have papers for you to sign and we will be on our way." Henry heard the front door open, "Who in the hell is that?" "Hello, Aunt Clara where are you? it's your favorite nephew I'm here to take you out to lunch just as I promised. HELLO, HELLO I saw you pull into the garage as I was driving up the drive… (silence) I'm coming up the stairs did you forget our date?"

Henry, "Who the frigging is this asshole? he will screw up the entire scam. Do you want me to take him out permanently or just knock the sucker out till we finish our business?"

Jimmy reached into his briefcase and pulled out two face masks a pouch of powder, "Here quickly put on one of these masks, Miss Clara go to the door and call your nephew up stairs. Tell him you have someone you want him to meet, do it now". "Henry when he opens the door step back and let me take over." Jimmy opens the pouch of powder and pours some of it in his gloved hand. "Andrew I am in the office up stairs please come up stairs I have someone I would like you to meet." Her nephew bounded up the stairs Henry opened the door as he entered the office. Jimmy blew the powder into his face and Andrew stopped dead in his tracks, standing there with a glazed look in his eyes. "WOW, that shit is the cats meow, where did you get hold of something like that? Jesus, Jimmy you are a wish and a wonder. Now what do we do with this bozo?". "We have him sign the papers as a witness that will make our claim iron clad. She wouldn't have a leg to stand on. "When the signing was complete," Andrew I want you to return to your car drive downtown have lunch. You will only remember that you witnessed the signing of your Aunts papers. You will have no memory of meeting Henry or myself, do you understand?", "Yes I understand, will have lunch now."

Jimmy flipped open Miss Clara's computer and punched in her Bank Account number, put the transfer code and within seconds five hundred thousand dollars was deposited in the Island Account when the transfer was complete took a hammer destroyed the hard drive. Jimmy, "Henry we are all done here she has twenty thousand in cash, here's five for you to play with. The rest is our living money till I set up another score you Miss Clara are very tired and need to go to bed we were never here." Miss Clara, "Yes, I am very tired I need to lay down rest for awhile."

CHAPTER: NINETEEN

etective Frank Jacobs was sitting at his desk when his phone rang, he picked up, "This is the Captain I just received a phone call from a Nursing Home they have an elderly woman that claims a pair of con men robbed her of her life savings." Jacobs, "Ok, what does that have to do with my case?"

"Her description of the them fits the two you and Jack have been chasing for the last six months. She is in a Nursing Home on the East Side. Jack is checking out a scam in Cleveland so I need you to step in and check it out. Her name is Mrs. Leo she is waiting for someone from the Station to take a statement". "Maybe we finally have a break in this case."

When he arrived at the Nurses Station he showed his badge asked for Mrs. Leo. "I'll call the Nurse that is tending to her. She will show you to the room, also her son, and daughter in law want to speak to you." "No problem, the more the merrier." He followed the Nurse, "If you don't mind I would like to question her without witnesses." Detective Jacobs entered the room introduced himself, "Hi, Mrs. Leo my name is Detective Jacobs I'm here to take you statement". "Yes officer anything you want." Frank, placed a recorder on the table started to question Mrs. Leo," Could you please give me your full name, address, how long you have lived at your last address, age, what does your children have to do with this?"

Mrs. Leo, "I received a call a few months ago by someone called James K. He said that my bank where I have my accounts with had advised him to call me and see if I was interested in setting up a retirement account that would net me six to ten percent a year tax free. I said yes. That would allow me to live quite comfortably with my husbands pension and Social Security, so I said yes."

Frank, "And then what happened, did he come to your house?"

Mrs. Leo, "He set up an appointment while we had our first meeting he was quite curious concerning the antiques and paintings in the house he recommended cataloguing them for insurance purposes. Plus it would be much easier for my son if for some reason he would have to take over my estate."

Frank, "Was that the last time you saw him?"

Mrs. Leo, "No, because of his incessant calling I agreed to let him come to the house to catalogue my antiques and paintings."

Frank, "You let him come to the house then what happened?"

Mrs. Leo, "He arrives with this Troll who calls calls me upstairs to look at a painting the next thing I know I am in the hospital, then some Nursing Home. I swear my Doctor was in league with them. He force fed me drugs that kept me comatose hoping to cause me brain damage."

She continued with her story her son and daughter in law had been working in Europe and when they returned found that my home had been sold, my whereabouts were unknown. They hired a Private Detective who traced me to the Nursing Facility. They arrived at the Nursing Facility with two Police Officers and demanded I be released immediately threatened to sue the Facility, my attending Physician. He had been administering mind altering drugs. My son had me transferred to this Home to recover. I am an elderly woman, those drugs could have permanently damaged my mind, I guess I am not as fragile as I once thought. Those two have left me penniless except for my Social Security and Pension. Detective Frank Jacobs, "That is quite a story do you think you could recognize the men who robbed you? I have a mug book I would like you to look through if you see anyone that looks familiar let me know."

He slid over a portable table laid the open Mug Book on it. "Don't forget if you see anyone of their pictures just point to the picture, I will take it from there." Mrs. Leo spent a few minutes looking through the book she turned every page to the end started flipping the pages backwards, half way through pointed to a sketch of James K., then a sketch of Henry turned the next page pointed to a third picture. "Thats the Doctor at the Nursing Facility he was a real quack if I were younger I would go after him myself". "Are you sure these are the men?" "Yes, they are the two at the house, that is the Doctor at the Home." Detective Frank Jacobs dialed his phone, "Send a squad car to the Nursing Facility where Mrs.Leo was found and bring Dr. Stimpson in for questioning." That evening he sent all the information to Morrison at the Police Department. Lieutenant Jack Morrison read the report the next morning thinking, "There is much more going on than meets the eye." There's Jimmy and Henry in league with Marjorie Swift robbing the homes of the rich she shorts whoever is her boss. Carl puts a price on her head, it appears tried to kill her she defends herself disappears God knows where. Now these same two lowlifes are bilking the elderly out of their retirement money, it disappears into an off Shore Account somehow this is all connected. He called the Cleveland Police Department and left a message for Sergeant Michaels, "Have to return to Los Angeles there has been a break in my LA investigation, will send you the evidence necessary to pursue the case."

CHAPTER: TWENTY

Morrison called Frank Jacobs Monday morning, "Can you have Mrs. Leo's son come to the station tomorrow at noon we have to figure out how these two are getting away with bilking people out of their savings."

They all sat down together brain storming, Morrison led, "How did they get your mother to sign the papers allowing for the legal sale of her home. Did they forge the documents? we need a handwriting expert to check over the paper work. Jimmy and Henry are experts at what they do I will give them that. If your lawyer can prove forgery or coercion the buyer of the home will have to relinquish title to the property. Maybe we can track down the antiques and paintings and have them returned."

Frank, "What if the present owners file a lawsuit to keep title to the property and how did they have the money released from the bank?"

Morrison, "Let me take care of the buyers when I get done with them they will step back and relinquish title guaranteed."

Frank, "I have a feeling we are onto something, my feeling is it is world wide." Morrison, "I agree this shit has been going on for quite a while I wouldn't be surprised if there isn't drugs and white slavery involved. We appear to have an Underground Mafia at work." He opened his note book and wrote the Bank's name and address, put the sketches out on an "All Points Bulletin" using the known names of the perpetrators, "thinking maybe we can get lucky" interview the new owners of Mrs. Leo's home and track down everyone who bought the paintings and antiques. See if there have been any assaults on women matching the prior rapes. Placed all of the evidence on the bulletin board for all to see. Then It occurred to him, "Why did Mrs. Leo call Henry a little Troll, I'll have to ask her what there was about him that prompted the description?"

He sat back staring at the board, these guys are always moving, they never seemed to stay in one place more than a month or two. Just enough time to set up residence, produce the necessary paper work, meet the pigeon, bilk them out of their money, sell off the property and disappear showing up a thousand miles away to start the scam all over again. They definitely were part of a larger organization.

Morrison called the home buyers,"Hello, I would like to visit and ask a few questions about who contacted you concerning your purchase of Mrs. Leo's home, who completed the legal documents for the sale?, What you don't want any frigging cops in your house. I'm very sorry but there is an ongoing investigation the sale of the home was a fraud you and your wife are both involved if you keep giving name a hard time I will have a warrant issued charging you with accepting stolen property or I could charge you with Grand Theft and impersonation. All I'm asking you is to let me come to your home and interview you. Yes, you can have a lawyer present, you know what I will see you at the station tomorrow morning at eight o'clock in the morning. If you don't show up I will issue a warrant and bring you in handcuffs."

Morrison slams down the phone, "God damned idiots they are going to call the Mayor. I don't care if they call the Pope they better be here at eight or I will personally issue a warrant."

One of the other officers commented, "Gees Morrison, you are really on a roll I thought you were going to rip him another one is this about those assaults?". "Yea, their getting to me those bastards are as slippery as eels but I am getting to understand how they think. Now I have to figure out where they will show up next to pull their scam."

Morrison was sitting at his desk at seven thirty the next morning, his phone rang at exactly eight after the second ring he picked it up," There's a couple here with their lawyer to see you, you want me to send them up?". "No, send them to interrogation and I will be right there and make sure they are comfortable get them coffee and donuts." Morrison I'll let them stew first soften them up. He waited twenty minutes then made his entrance opening the door with a bang everyone in the room jumped giving a startled look, he loved throwing his prey off guard even the lawyer looked uneasy. "Hello, I'm lieutenant Morrison sorry to keep you waiting."

He placed a tape recorder on the table, "I would appreciate it if when you answer questions you speak up, I wouldn't want to have to call you in for a second time to clarify your answers. That would be very bothersome for all of us, would you please state your names, addresses, what you do for a living, age, how you came to purchase Mrs. Leo's home, Real estate Agent and did you have a personal relationship with the Realtor?"

"Our names are Mr. and Mrs. Jones, we are self employed Art Dealers, no we do not have a personal relationship with the Realtor. Her name is Rose Cannon she had our name because we were looking for a home in this particular neighborhood and why would we be charged with fraud we did noting wrong?" Morrison threw a half a dozen questions at the couple hoping to catch them in a lie, "The sale of the house was based on fraud. So I will tell you what will probably happen, I don't know how much money you put down to buy the house. If I were you I would talk to the bank and see if you can talk them into returning your deposit, why did you buy this particular property?" Husband, "The price was thirty percent under the normal asking price for this area. We were told that an old woman in a Nursing Home needed the money so we jumped at the deal. Our lawyer at the closing said it was a good deal and we had saved ourselves a good chunk of change. I guess a so called good deal can come back and bite you in the ass."

Morrison, "I need the name of your lawyer and any paper work relevant to the closing. I am sorry you were scammed but we have been chasing these "Fraudsters" all over the country. The real owners Lawyer has already notified the bank about the scams. Word to the wise I believe the bank doesn't want it's name connected to the con, if you press hard enough they will give you your down payment back. Closing costs I doubt they will return. Please send me your new address I may need you as material witnesses, have a nice day." The Lawyer looked at the couple, "What just happened? It's all said and done, that Detective is one smooth talker." He walked back to his office and told one of the clerks, "Find the phone number for a Realtor named Rose Cannon I want her in my office this afternoon or tomorrow morning at the latest." Clerk, "The Realtor will be here tomorrow at nine, said she had an early showing and will be here with the paper work for the sale." At nine on the dot Rose Cannon walked into the Police Station and asked for Lieutenant Morrison. She was escorted to his office, he waved her to a chair. "Miss Rose Cannon?" "Yes that's my name". "Who gave you the right to sell Mrs. Leo's home and why did it sell so cheap, were you in with the seller who perpetrated this fraud, were you aware of the circumstances leading up to the sale?" She was a cool customer, Rose just sat there and let Morrison run out of questions before she answered him, "I have a legal bill of sale, the gentleman who acted as agent for the owner. He had all the necessary paper work and Power of Attorney to act in her stead. I even went to her Nursing Home to confirm her condition. Mrs. Leo was incapacitated she couldn't even tell me her name so there didn't appear to be any fraud involved. This Jimmy K. knew just what to say and do. He ordered me to sell the house at thirty percent below market value and I would be paid double commission. Jimmy said the owner needed the money to pay her bills so I sold the house, what did you expect me to do?" Morrison just sat there listening she had all the answers, he didn't even have to question her, she went on, "I do understand the buyers are screwed, I will give up my commission, which is the shits but life is life. You have to bend over once in awhile. Anything else you want to know? here is all the paper work from the sale. I have another meeting in an hour so if you have anymore questions call me on my cell phone and I will gladly try to help." Miss Rose Cannon stood up and waved him a salute and exited the office not looking back.

Morrison, "What in the hell just happened? she was good real good I should call her back in for questioning just for the hell of it. She probably kick my butt", and laughed. He opened the file she had left on his desk, everything she had mentioned was in the file, there was the power of attorney she even had it witnessed by her lawyer and he said everything appeared to be in order. After Morrison reviewed the file he called down to the Forensics Lab, "Can you send someone to my office I have paperwork that I want checked for fingerprints and DNA. If you could have the lab work complete as soon as possible I would be very appreciative."

"Hey Morrison you have a call on line one a Mr. Jones wants to speak to you". "I wonder if he is going to give me a bunch of bull, hello Mr. Jones what can I do for you today, you don't say. ("The bank gave you back your down payment and canceled the mortgage and you appreciate my advice"), well I am glad to be of service, yes if I have anymore questions I will be sure to call."He hung up the phone thinking, "Well I'll be damned someone actually thanked me, that is a first. I need a drink."

Opened the bottom drawer of his desk and pulled out a bottle of twelve year old Bourbon unscrewed the cap and poured himself three fingers. Sat back in his chair and sipped the nectar enjoying the sensation of of the Bourbon on his palate. He was getting nearer to catching those two jokers, they were just the tip of the Iceberg. "When I break this case I'm going to get a promotion and a raise. This case is deep very deep I'll have to watch my back wouldn't be surprised if there won't be a price on my head." They will be writing about this case in the Police Gazette. "Enough of this Morrison you have a long way to go before this case is solved and put to bed."

CHAPTER: TWENTY ONE

She stood looking at the old homestead thinking, "It will take me at least a couple of months to get this place livable. No one has lived here for five years. None of my siblings are interested in the Homestead so all the repairs will be on me. What a mess the house is infested with mice and squirrels they have to be my first priority. My second is the barn I called a local carpenter to give me a price on fixing the roof on the barn and house, it needs new windows before winter sets in. She donned her Muk Luks, covered her upper torso with a large bear skin coat, stepped out into the front yard, it felt good she had been away for way too long. Raised her head sniffing the clean air of the wilderness, gave the neighborhood a long howl. Then crouching into an attack position growled her eyes closing into points of grey light, "These are my people and this is my land anyone who trespasses these Sacred Borders will regret the day they were born. I will put you into your grave and you will disappear from the face of the earth never to be found again."

She could feel in her inner being that they would be coming for her. That stupid Morty never knew to just leave well enough alone. He had to try and erase any chance of someone spilling the beans, when she took care of the hit men Morty would be next on the list I will make him rue the day that slimy lawyer was born. "Do I want to just burn him alive or better yet set him up so he is put away for a long, long time." Walked to her truck and opened a box containing cameras and looked around her property, "Four on the barn, a half a dozen on the house and a dozen installed in the woods. I want a three hundred and sixty degrees of cover. Cameras on all four corners of the house, the barn, the road leading to the property and a few in the woods."

Spent the next week preparing for the killers she knew would surely be coming take her out. On the path to the house she used a backhoe to dig pits every thirty feet and installed sharpened steel rods, concealed the traps with a canvas covering, then she placed a few inches of earth for camouflage. All through the woods encircling the property she placed trip wires with with grenades hidden in cans and finally Tiger Traps and a concealed tripwire that would cause the hidden stake to impale the intruders. Finally when everything was complete she stepped back to admire her handy work, she thanked the Metis People who had helped her in the task, "Chief, I thank you and your people for your help but you must go now I don't want anyone hurt or killed I can handle this from here." She was half Metis a little known tribe in Canada that was a mix of French and Cree peoples recognized by the Canadian Government. She shook hands and told them to return to their tribe she didn't want them involved in her battles. Some time passed and one day while she was in town shopping at a local store noticed a couple of men walking down the street taking pictures, they had the look of Mercenaries, brawny, wide shoulders, they were carrying, asking questions. She entered the town

Lodge and questioned the clerk, "I noticed a couple of men down the street I wonder just what their business is in town?". "They are here to hunt". "Hunt what? the deer season isn't for two weeks". "They said they arrived early to learn where the best hunting and looking for a guide". "Very interesting I thank you for the information. OH, by the way have they asked about anyone living in the village". "Why yes someone named Marjorie Swift, apparently the very tall gentleman is a long lost relative". "and what was your reply?". "That there used to be a family by that name living up river near the Metis Reservation." Marjorie had taken the precaution of dressing as a Metis Squaw, dying her hair black. Marjorie watched as ten more strangers infiltrated the village asking questions as to where they could find a place to room further up river in the interior. She accosted one of the visitors speaking mix of English and Metis language, "I hear you are looking for a place to stay, how long are you here for, how many people will be looking for shelter?". "We will be here for two weeks and need a place to lay our heads when we are not hunting, it has to be cleared so we can park our vehicles." Marjorie, "Where are you from you'r not Canadian?" Mercenary, "From allover!". "I can probably set you up in a cabin a few miles drive North of here. The cabin is owned by a white woman." She saw a look on his face that told her he heard what he was looking for. "Really, can you give me directions to to the cabin we will gladly pay the owner anything she asks. I will tell the others and we can proceed tomorrow morning. What do you say can I get you to guide us?". "I must ask my husband for permission but if he say I no can go I will leave directions at the Lodge. Have to go now to make food for my family." He was a big man lean all muscle, about six foot three inches, weight two hundred forty pounds.

Mercenary, "He wondered why they needed so many ex-mercenaries to take out one woman, when one or two snipers could do the job. All they had was a picture of the prey, they were not given any reason for her assassination." Orders were just do it, and bring back proof of her death preferably her head. They appeared to be scared shitless of her, wanted her dead afraid she would give up their secrets and the money they were being paid was beyond belief.

"Ok Guys, we move in the morning. I have directions to our quarry, pack up the gear and make sure all the weapons are cleaned and ready. Jerry, take the trucks and fill them with gas and all of our spare gas cans. Mack, go to the local store and buy beef jerky and any food that will keep, have the vehicles ready for five tomorrow morning."

Marjorie headed North as soon as she was out of the Mercenaries sight, made sure to leave directions at the Lodge to her place.

"I need to be there tonight to set the booby traps and Tiger Pits, so everything is ready to welcome them. When I am done with those bastards I will make sure that the California Mob never bothers me again. The ones I don't kill I will put away for a long time. They are screwing with the wrong lady."

The men slowly infiltrating the Village had been noticed by the local Police Force, they didn't fit the profile of the typical touristy hunter. They were all well built, had the look of EX-Military. The local Police had alerted Canada's CSIS that there could be a terrorist threat of some magnitude about to be committed. The CSIS was monitoring their phone calls but the head of the group had an encrypted phone that they couldn't break into, this made them more suspicious as to their being in the village which was a very soft target or something more insidious. Their rooms were searched while they were in the local Pub drinking. They found bullet proof vests, night goggles, grenades, and automatic weapons. This group was ready to make war. It was decided to keep them under surveillance and if they even looked the wrong way they would be taken out of commission. So far except for a couple of them getting drunk they had kept their noses clean and had not committed any crimes.

At five in the morning they were observed loading their vehicles, driving North out of town. The Authorities were still in the dark. One of the officers went to the Lodge and asked the clerk if he had any idea where the hunters were going. "Why yes, a woman from the Metis Tribe had left directions to a cabin a couple hours drive north, she said to make sure they didn't leave without the directions because they would never find the cabin without them."

"Did you happen to overhear exactly what they were here for? the hunting season doesn't start for two weeks. We have reason to believe they are here for some other reason than hunting. We think they are terrorists or assassins they may want to take out our power grid or who knows what." Hotel Clerk, "The squaw left directions to the old Swift property no one has lived there for at least twenty years."

CHAPTER: TWENTY TWO

lerk, "I believe the last couple of months Charley Long Saw was fixing up the cabin, clearing out the brush, she had all the trees cut down within one hundred yards of the house. I heard Charley Long Saw say she had him fix up the roof and install new windows maybe she is the target, it doesn't make sense to me but maybe you should take a ride up to the Swift place and check it out."

"Slow down Benny you will get us all killed before we ever get to the cabin. I want to sneak up on her our client said do not under estimate our target she has military training and will use it if she has any idea that she is under threat. So stay cool and keep the speed under fifty miles an hour."

"OK Boss, I just get all juiced up when we go for a kill even if it is some broad I like to see them squirm before I give the target a head shot". "Benny you are a homicidal maniac, that is why they gave you a medical discharge you just like to kill and they were afraid you would take it out on your own people, so be cool you will get your chance at the quarry."

As they approached within a mile of the cabin he signaled Benny to slow down to a crawl. He didn't want to alert the target he wanted to take her by surprise crash into the cabin and put a bullet in her forehead before she had a chance to make a break for it. They were in sight of the prey when suddenly there was a loud "SCREECH" as the front of the leading Vehicle disappeared into the earth, immediately followed by sound of hidden metal spears tipped with armor piercing rounds exploded penetrating the underside of the Jeep causing a gut wrenching explosion that ripped through the underside of the vehicle killing three of the occupants instantly. The vehicle burst into flames causing the two living survivors to roll out of the inferno with their clothes ablaze screaming for their comrades to "Have Mercy" they rolled on in the dirt trying to put out the searing flames, the napalm soaked into their clothes and when they ripped off whatever they were wearing the skin peeled off their bodies layer by layer, the last words heard, "please help us."

Phil, "Don't sit on your dumb asses staring grab a couple of extinguishers and put out their burning clothes. Too late Phil they are both dead. What the frigging was that? the bitch knew we were coming and sent us a message, don't screw with me. Now she will die slowly, very slowly!!". "Everyone leave the vehicles where they are and spread out along the perimeter". "Ignamar load the rocket launcher and level that fucking cabin. I want the place destroyed. I am sure she knows we are here by now as a matter a fact every living creature within five miles heard the explosion of the Jeep."

Boss, "We have to get the hell out of here that Jeep is loaded with ammo. We need to find cover before it takes out the rest of us." They all ran a few hundred yards and took cover behind any thing they could. The explosion lit up the sky and the ground shook the explosion could be heard for miles.

She stood on the hill with a smug look on her face, "You bastards have met your match there are at least seven of them left. That Morty didn't waste any expense to take me out. Now that they have tasted my booby traps they will be extremely careful." She headed for the backwoods her plan was to blend in with the locals. Marjorie was sure that her Tiger Traps would cripple or kill at least another two or three of her pursuers leaving about four that would still be tracking her. The copter was circling overhead when the Jeep plunged into the Tiger Trap there was a ball of fire that lit up the night. Copter Pilot "What in the hell was that?" Canadian Trooper, "Put eyes on the explosion, the road to the cabin is booby trapped, these assholes have a Tiger by the tail what ever they are being paid it isn't enough."

That Jeep just evaporated into a mound of molten metal, I can see two men rolling around on the ground with their clothes on fire. Radio the Rangers to take these guys down before it gets worse" "Jesus Christ, one of them just fired a rocket at the cabin." The words were no sooner out of his mouth when the cabin disappeared in a bright flash that lit up the night, debris covered the sky. "Get us out of here if they see us we will be dead men." She saw the Copter through the trees and signaled in Morse Code with her flashlight directing them to a safe landing site. The pilot read Marjorie's message and landed directly behind her on the hill she was standing on.

Copter Pilot, "Lady what in the hell is going on? they sent all of that fire power to take out one person and it's a woman on top of it. You sure must have made some extremely powerful enemies."

Marjorie, "Don't go near the barn or the Cabin I have grenades and trip wires all around the building perimeters. To be safe I would wait a few more minutes till a few more of the Mercenaries are either wounded or killed. Then they will be more willing to surrender they work for pay and don't normally feel it's enough to die for, they thought I was a soft target." As they were talking there was a scream, "OH My GOD! my leg it's gone please help me put a bullet in my head. I surrender." "Well there goes another one there's maybe four active shooters left. I would appreciate it if you could round them up before they take my barn out". "Lady I don't know who you are but you are one cold babe, I wouldn't want to meet you in a dark alley." Anyone else would be having a heart attack but you stand here as blasé as can be. I wouldn't want to get on your bad side so what do we do with the ones still living."

CHAPTER: TWENTY THREE

arjorie turned with a smirk on her face, "That's your call I would charge the entire lot with Domestic Terrorism put them in jail and throw away the key, sounds good to me."

A back up force of Canadian Federal Police had surrounded the remaining Mercenaries. She gave them the coordinates of the remaining traps and helped neutralize them so no one else would be wounded or killed.

Captain of the Federal Police, "We have them all rounded up the only one missing is the one named Benny. I guess he is the worst of the lot one of the prisoners said he is a stone cold killer. We'll bring in some police dogs tomorrow and track him down we can't allow some nut case to run loose in the woods God knows what he will do if we don't catch him. He will either surrender or I will have the bastard put down."

The Canadian Police placed Marjorie on a copter and put her under protective custody at a secure facility hundreds of miles from the original crime scene. The Authorities felt he would come back to her place to complete the job and collect the bounty.

They asked the CIA if they could have one of their Spy Satellites positioned to keep an eye on the property.

"We have a number of Mercenaries in custody that appear to be associated with an American Hate Group. We have everyone except for one I will send you his profile."

When the Canadian Police sent Bennies profile to the CIA and they entered his information in their computer data base he immediately popped up listed as a Domestic Terrorist wanted in half a dozen states for bank robberies and murder. It appeared Benny was a real bad boy and a busy one. When the Canadian Police asked the four men in custody what they knew about Benny? They answered that he was part of the team that's all they know.

The Captain of the Canadian Police, "We have four of them in custody I want them separated put them in cells with a snitch. We can hold them for seventy two hours before we have to bring them before a judge who hopefully won't let them out on Bail or we can turn them over to the FBI on charges of Domestic Terrorism as they are American citizens even though the crime was committed in Canada against a citizen with dual citizenship in both countries. Also it appears an American citizen who resides in the state of California initiated an assassination in a foreign country, extremely complicated case."

One of the Officers sent Marjorie's information to the FBI and CIA it came back Top Secret need to know our eyes only.

Boss, "We have a Bolo on our Marjorie Swift the FBI wants us to hold her in custody till they can pick her up. It seems she has information on an ongoing murder case, etc, etc!"

Captain, "I wonder what she knows that is worth a million dollar hit and hiring ten Mercenaries to do the job. This whole scenario is something out of a spy novel."

The FBI arrived the next day the Canadian Authorities turned over the four prisoners, they were loaded into an Armor Plated Van and Marjorie was escorted back to the states in an SUV.

The four were whisked to the nearest airport, there they boarded a plane and upon landing disappeared into the Federal Judicial System to be questioned, FBI Agent, "What do they know?". "Not much their Boss was contacted by a go between, offered a hundred thousand each man and a million dollars when they had her head for proof of death. Never met, everything was completed over the internet". "Just keep them isolated till we can find out what this is all about."

Meanwhile Benny was running loose in the Canadian backwoods. "I will kill the bitch myself and collect the million dollar bounty on her head, those bastards have been trying to track me down for the last two weeks lots of luck. I have to find out where they are keeping her the FBI must have a Safe House somewhere in the Village." He had spent two weeks in the backwoods, grown a beard and had not washed in weeks. "I must smell real ripe so most people will give me a wide berth when I'm around, with my beard and long hair they will have a hard time recognizing me."

He entered the Village when the sun went down and acted like a homeless person by rummaging through dumpsters. Benny, "I saw my brothers taken away in handcuffs and leg irons. The FBI treated them like vermin. We just do what we are paid to do we are all ex-military." On one of his nightly trips he overheard the local Police they wanted him dead or alive.

There was a ten thousand dollar award on his head and apparently there was a murder warrant for murder one in Texas.

"That is a crock the stupid cowboy tried to smash my head with a crow bar but my reflexes were faster than his and I opened him up with my knife. He bled to death before I could stop the bleeding he was a stupid, drunk. Then there were the the stolen cars and the Police chase in California the Police chase car overturned and burst into flames and the Police almost burned to death. They just are out to get me I don't do nothing wrong but they just won't leave me alone. I have checked all over this town and still can't figure out where they stashed that broad haven't seen hide or hair of her since the FBI placed her in custody. I'm damned tired of been hanging around smelly garbage dumpsters. I will find her or they will either kill or capture me. I sure as hell am not going back to Texas to be convicted of murder and put in the gas chamber." Benny, "Screw them I will go down in a gun fight they will never take me alive."

Sergeant Murphy of the Canadian Royal Police, "We still haven't caught sight of this Benny character. The scuttle butt is Marjorie Swift is here in a safe house, hopefully Benny will take the bait. I will bet he is hanging around the Village, from his MO, he is like a bulldog I think he is looking for our lady friend, he wants to collect that million dollar bounty. He doesn't know that she is long gone to the states and being protected by the FBI in a safe house. Keep your eyes peeled this creep would think nothing of killing a cop or two. We need to plant a couple of our people undercover a female and a male officers dressed as street people, maybe we can smoke him out."

"Tell officer Tracey and officer Mc Connell to come to my office in the morning and I will brief them on how to dress and where to look for our elusive Mr. Benny. I have been talking to a number of people in town and from their description he has been spotted lurking around the fringes of the Village business area at night."

Officer Tracy, "He has grown a beard and wears ratty clothes that make him look like a beggar. The Captain has given everyone a warning to keep their distance he is definitely a very dangerous individual. We are told to shadow him, find out where he sleeps and take him when he least expects it."

Officer Mc Connell, "How in the hell did I deserve this duty? I never went undercover in my entire career. How about you Tracy what did you do to get picked?"

"I don't mind, we could get promotions if we capture this nut ball. He is one dangerous hombre so be careful they think he is prowling around the Village looking for Marjorie Swift to kill her and collect the million dollar bounty, only she is long gone back to the states protected by the FBI."

Mc Connell, "I will start on the west side of town dressed like a hobo so I can fit in when I go dumpster diving, we both will be wearing wires hopefully the info we have on his movements will bear fruit. I don't relish walking around looking for the creep."

She laughs, "I will start on the east side dressed like a hooker wearing a red dress, high heels and a wire. There will be plain clothes Detectives staked out around town just in case we encounter Benny and he starts to run or worse."

The first night he took the West side and she patrolled the East, they walked the streets till dawn but found no sign of Benny. The next night Mc Connell spotted a figure in the back of the Police Station, "You, halt Police," the figure disappeared around the back of the Station. Mc Donnell took off running and with his gun drawn ran toward the figure but when he turned the corner the shadow was gone, "I'll be a son of a bitch, I saw him I know it was Benny. What's he doing prowling around the Police Station? and then he disappears."

He calls for backup, "Hey guys send a car around the back of the Station, see if there is someone walking or hiding in the shadows. I swear I spotted him and then he was gone. Don't take any chances he is armed and an ex-Seal so be very careful." "Hey Tracey, I saw him near the Police Station so keep an eye out he may be coming your way the bastard is like a puff of smoke here one minute gone the next."

She stepped back into the shadows of a door way to let her eyes acclimate to the night and stood there holding her breath. Tracey, "Holy Shit, I think I just saw him across the street he is moving pretty fast, has he spotted you?". "I'm at Broad and Walnut hiding in a doorway I don't think he's seen me. You better move on him now or you will loose him."

Benny, "I could feel cops eyes on me they have plain clothes cops on the street. Someone must have recognized me and told the Police." At least I am still wearing my Bullet Proof Vest and carrying my automatic pistol" the UZI he had buried in the woods where he was hiding out during the day but that was on the other side of town he had to find someplace to disappear they had him cornered and he would have to have a shoot out with the Police. Bennie quickly glanced up looking for a sniper he knew would be scoping him out looking to do a head shot.

Just then a light caught his eye there was someone leaving a store. It was three in the morning. Benny acted with out thinking, grabbed the old man who was probably the owner, put a gun to his head, "Keep your mouth shut and I will let you live get back inside, close the door, lie down on the floor, put your hands behind your back." He pulled out a pair of zip handcuffs, he had the old man cuffed before he knew what was going on.

"Where does the back door lead to old man? answer me straight I don't want to have to come back and put a bullet in the back of your head, so don't bullshit me and I won't hurt you."

"The back door leads to an alley and if you turn left it will lead you straight into the woods. Please don't hurt me I'm just an old man and would like to live a few more years to enjoy my grandchildren."

When he looked up the figure in black had disappeared. He thought if it wasn't for the cuffs he must have been imagining things in his old age. Tracey, "SHIT, where did he vanish to? I turned just for a second to stay in the shadows so I wouldn't be spotted and puff he is gone, this guy is a real spook. I say converge on the area he must still be here somewhere." She could see a light on in the Second Hand Store across the street maybe he went into the store and exited through the rear. She ran across the street to the store and glanced inside, there on the floor was a figure that appeared to be in distress. Tracey called for backup, "I need backup at the Second Hand Store there is someone laying on the floor and he looks as if he is cuffed, please respond ASAP!"

Officer Mc Connell, "Will be there in less than five, keep an eye on the victim if necessary break the glass on the front door especially if he appears to be in distress."

She looked up and could see flashing lights coming down the street. "Ok Tracey, give me a second and I will pick the lock. I've sent another car around back to check out the alley." They entered the store with guns drawn just in case it was an ambush, once in the store she cut off the cuffs and rolled the victim over it was Mr. Philip the store owner. He sat up and rubbed his wrists, "Thank you very much I thought the man in black was going to kill me, he asked me where the back door would lead to, he said answer truthfully or I will blow your head off. I told him it would allow him to escape into the woods, he cuffed me and was gone before I knew it."

CHAPTER: TWENTY FOUR

"The sunrise is in a couple of minutes, I'll call out the copter to survey the area if he's headed for the woods it's at least a mile before the canopy becomes impenetrable maybe we can cut him off before he disappears into the forest?"

By the time the copter arrived overhead Bennie was long gone. He had broken into a run as soon as he exited the building.

His Seal training had taught him to run like hell, in less than five minutes he reached the tree line and kept that pace for another twenty minutes.

"Sergeant be very cautious, we believe he is well armed with an automatic weapon and will use it if cornered. I would deploy the men on the perimeter of the woods till the copter has a chance to see if they can at least pick up a heat source."

The Police waited an hour, no heat source, he had just disappeared everyone just scratched their heads. "Keep looking the dogs will be here within the hour the bastard must be holed up in a cave." They let the dogs loose, "Lets go they have his scent we have him now." After a couple of hours the dogs were going in circles they had lost his scent.

One of the handlers picked up a broken limb that appeared to have been cut on purpose. "What in the hell is that smell? It's creosote they use it to keep railroad ties from rotting. This is what is throwing the dogs off his scent he may have put some of it on his clothes." Bennie, "The stupid cops are looking for me in the woods I just went in far enough for the dogs to pick up my scent then sprayed myself with creosote. They don't know I backtracked and hot wired a truck an hour ago and I'm heading South out of Canada." He stayed on the logging road as long as he could. When he ran out of gas. Bennie, "Now what the hell do I do with the truck?" spied a steep ravine and rolled the truck down it, throwing his weapons after the truck, keeping only the Special Forces Tactical Knife hidden in his boot.

Sitting in the woods watching the human defile her forest was a large Black Bear. She just sat silently and stared as the human all dressed in black trudged away to the South at least he wouldn't be of any danger to her cubs. Because she would have had to kill the intruder.

Bennie walked till nightfall. Climbed a large tree that had branches strong enough to hold a man to use as a place to lay his head for the night. He lashed himself to the bough so as not to fall the forty feet to the ground as he slept, in the morning he would continue his journey South, "Those cops will never catch me, I would bet they are still looking for me in the back woods."

CHAPTER: TWENTY FIVE

Lieutenant Morrison had run into a Dead End, the attacks on women had ceased and the Bunko schemes on older couples to bilk them out of their estates had also come to a stand still.

He decided to send a query to the local Police in bordering states to see if he could scare up anything that caught his eye. The Sunday paper was laying on his desk, he hadn't read a newspaper in a couple of weeks so he sat down to peruse through it nothing really seemed to grab his interest and he folded the paper and was about to throw it in the trash when a quirky story caught his eye. There was a story about an elderly woman and her nephew who under the influence of some sort of drug had her sign over her entire estate to someone called James K. with her nephew as a witness to the transaction. This occurred in an upscale area of Chicago. This James K. had an accomplice who fit the description of Henry. The story also went on to elaborate that the state Forensics Lab is still trying to track down the drug. They think it is grown somewhere in South America but cannot find where it actually originated.

Morrison re-read the article again, "I know they are the perps I am looking for, Hey Maggie, can you get me the phone number of Chicago's River North Station I think I have a lead on those two con artists."

Maggie I have them on the phone, "Hello, this is Lieutenant Morrison from the Los Angeles police department can I speak to the head of your bunko squad. It is very important please have him call me back I think I have a lead on the people who robbed a Miss Clara. They have been traveling around the country bilking people out of their inheritance and life savings, I will wait in my office for his call, thanks."

He was sitting at his desk when the phone rang, "Hello this is Lieutenant Morrison". "This is Sergeant Logan head of the bunko squad in Chicago returning your call. My secretary said you may have a lead on the Miss Clara case."

"To start I read an article in Chicago paper where an elderly woman was robbed by a gentlemen named James K. Would it be possible for me to come to Chicago and interview the victim? I have been tracking this suspect from Los Angeles to Cleveland and now it appears he has struck in the Chicago area. I also suspect he has a partner that has committed a number of sexual assaults on young women, if you don't mind I will send over artists sketches of the suspects. They have been identified by a number of victims in our area."

Sergeant Logan, "Sounds good we could use your help."

"I'll be in Chicago in the morning. No need to pick me up I will rent a car and if you can have Miss Clara and her nephew in your office in the morning I would like to interview them concerning how she met this James K. there seems to be some connection between him and a burglary ring in California. Will see you about ten in the morning. I will have my secretary email you everything I have this afternoon."

His plane landed at eight the next morning he had his secretary make a copy of the files so he could review them while questioning the victim who had been duped and her nephew, Morrison couldn't figure how he was involved in this mess.

The rental car was waiting at the airport exit to the terminal it had a GPS as he requested. The drive to the Police Station took an hour, parked and grabbing his briefcase bounded up the stairs, stopped at the desk, "Can you guide me to Sergeant Logan's office". "Are you Morrison?". "Yes". "He's waiting for you in the conference room on the second floor please follow me." Morrison entered the conference room and laid down his briefcase shook hands with Sergeant Logan, without stopping to take a breath continued, "Morrison here, how are you Sergeant and I take it you are Miss Clara and this is your nephew. I read about your case in the newspaper. I asked Sergeant Logan to ask you here today because I believe your case is connected to a number of schemes that have been perpetrated on the elderly in the last few months." Sitting down at the table opened his briefcase and spread out the files, he showed them pictures of the two suspects. Morrison felt really sorry for Miss Clara as she was visibly upset and appeared on the verge of breaking down crying.

"Now, now Miss Clara can you identify these sketches are they the men who robbed you? please tell me in your own words how they contacted you and what did they do to get you to sign over your retirement funds to a complete stranger, just think take your time for a second before you answer."

Miss Clara, "I received a letter from what I thought was an investment company, the letter stated that they had a working relationship with my bank and if I invested with their company I would receive a minimum of twelve percent interest a year. I spoke to this James K. over the phone and he invited me to have lunch with him at an exclusive country club. He had a chauffeured Limousine pick me up at my residence. It all seemed up and up we had lunch and just before the meal was over I began to feel very strange. I could hear him speaking to me and whatever he ordered me to do I felt I had no choice but to obey. I entered the Limousine and I was driven back to my house, papers were placed in front of me and I was told to sign. I think at this point my nephew arrived and confronted them. This James K. at this point blew some type of powder in his face and my nephew was commanded to witness the signing of the documents after the signing he ordered my nephew to drive downtown and buy himself some lunch. That is all I remember till I went to the bank to withdraw money from my account and was told that the account was empty. Someone had made a bank wire withdrawal from my account to a bank in the Islands and when I had the bank investigate where my money had been wired to it had disappeared from that bank into who knows where, so Detective that is my story they conned me out of one million two hundred thousand dollars. I hope you find them and put them away for a long time."

Morrison interviewed the nephew and he confirmed the entire story. He wondered what was the powder they claimed caused them to loose their will and follow any command that James K. ordered,

"I will definitely look into this", He looked at Miss Clara, "Have you cleaned up your study where the documents were signed?". "Heavens no, the desk hasn't been touched it's just as we left it". "Good, don't touch a thing there may still be traces of the powder on the desk or somewhere in the study. I will send a forensic team to the house and maybe they can ascertain where the powder originated, please bear with me for a little longer we will make you comfortable here while the team searches the house." Sergeant Logan picked up the phone, "How soon can we have a forensic team ready to proceed to Miss Clara's house? I want you to do a complete sweep of her house starting with the study. Myself and Lieutenant Morrison will accompany the team. We are leave immediately and I expect you will be right behind us, you do understand? very good I will see you at the house."

CHAPTER: TWENTY SIX

When they arrived at the home everyone donned Hazmat Gear and entered the house, the Team followed right behind the detectives.

Morrison, "Look for a white powder but keep any evidence in separate evidence bags don't mix it all together there may be more than one type of drug."

The team found three piles of white powder scattered around the upstairs office, now all they had to do was analyze what it was and where it came from. The Forensic Lab Team worked through the night, next morning Sergeant Logan had the report placed on his desk. Everyone wanted to know what the drug was that would make you into a zombie, "I think they had ulterior motives." Morrison's phone rang, "Hello Morrison, I have the results on my desk this powder is derived from a plant in Columbia, South America. It is called Scopolamine or Devils Breath the effects cause people to fall into a hypnotic trance, the victim will do as ordered for a short amount of time, too much and the victim can have a heart attack.

Where they purchased the drug is anyone's guess we definitely have a couple of Con men with a bag full of tricks."

Sergeant Logan, "Why don't we check out the Country Club and find out why they were allowed to use the Club as their staging ground."

Both of the Detectives drove to the Club, "Who plays good cop and who plays bad cop? I think it should be you Morrison your from out of town so any fallout will be on you and you will be long gone" Jones laughed.

Morrison, "Your a real peach maybe I can do the same for you some day."

They went to the main office, "We are looking for the General Manager". "and who may I say is asking?" they both showed her their badges, she immediately showed them to the managers office.

"Bob there's a couple of Detectives that would like to speak to you. If you need me I will be at my desk." "Yes officers, what can I do to help you? Please be brief I have a very hectic day ahead of me, we are catering two wedding rehearsals this afternoon and I am short on help."

Morrison, "I understand you allowed a James K. to utilize the Club for business purposes is that correct?"

"Why yes, I was approached by one of my waitresses that a James K. from California who was a member of a prestigious Country Club out west and he would appreciate it if he could bring a guest for lunch and he would pay the club a sum of one thousand dollars for the privilege. I called the named club and they said yes he was a member in good standing, so I agreed. What is the problem? after they had lunch he and the an older woman left in a Limousine."

"We would like to question the waitress is she on this shift?"

"Come to think of it the next day she called in sick and I haven't seen her since. She never even filled out her paperwork I don't know where she lives, that's quite strange."

The two Detectives looked at each other and shook their heads. "What a mess this is like trying to unravel a Chinese puzzle. There is no end to the characters in this play and it seems this is only the first act,Lord only knows when this will all end."

Just when they thought they had a strong lead it evaporated in a cloud of smoke.

"Do you still have the phone number for the club in California"
"Why yes I do, let me look on my desk I wrote it down on an envelope. AH! here it is I talked to the manager of the club and he assured me this James K. was a sterling member and would appreciate it if I could accommodate him, so I said yes."

Lieutenant Morrison dialed the number and received a message that it was no longer in service. He placed the phone in the cradle giving the manager a questioning look. The poor manager was about to dump in his pants, he started to stutter.

"I,…I…,I am positive that is the number I called information to confirm the phone number the waitress gave me was legitimate. I don't understand how this can be, please don't make a fuss I will lose my job, please I beg of you!!"

"Relax, we believe you somehow they rerouted the call to an accomplice on the outside who told you what you wanted to hear."

Sergeant Logan, "If you don't mind, when you are off work today I would appreciate your coming down to the station and working with our sketch artist to draw a sketch of the waitress. Maybe we can identify her, she may have a record I would like to see you there before four this afternoon,Yes."

"I will be there, I appreciate your not involving the club."

The Club manager was at the station at four sharp and gave a very good description of the waitress. Now If they could put a name to the sketch it would give them something too go on, so far James K. and Henry had disappeared. Those two were real slippery just like the eels they were, but sooner or later they would slip up and the Police would nail them now that they were on their tail. Plus the assaults on young women had ceased.

Morrison wondered what next? "I hope this Henry doesn't start murdering his victims or really maiming them, it's not unusual for someone like Henry to commit a more serious crime, the assaults are like a drug addict the perp needs something stronger to bring him to a climax."

CHAPTER: TWENTY SEVEN

Sergeant Logan, "We identified the waitress I posted the sketch on the board, one of the Officers that walks the beat downtown recognized her, she is a prostitute and has been hauled in a number of times for solicitation. Her name is Maizzie, I just sent a car down to see if she is selling and pick her up maybe we can squeeze some information out of her. So far we have a lot of questions but few answers."

Sergeant Logans phone rang, "What's up?". "She's down stairs in the interrogation room". "Good, let her stew for a couple of hours and turn up the heat so she will be in a literal sweat it will make her uncomfortable when I question her."

An hour later Sergeant Logan entered the interrogation room he had turned on the air conditioning, so now she was shivering. He just smiled and sat at the other side of the table and stared not saying a word.

Maizzie, "What the frig do you want with me I didn't do anything wrong are you trying to give me pneumonia? It's cold in here come on give me a break."

Sergeant Logan "How do you know Jimmy K., what part of the scam were you involved in, how much were you paid? who was on the other end of that phony phone number? you know we could charge you as an accessory, impersonation, etc, etc!!"

Maizzie, "Whoa Sarge, what in the hell are you talking about Jimmy gave me five hundred large to see if I could get a job as a waitress at the club. He gave me a phone number and explained how I should approach the manager and when. If I succeeded I would received another five hundred and that's the only skin I had in the game. I had not a clue what he was up to he never lets anyone in on his scams, he's one slick dude and good looking too I would give him some free without a second thought. How about you Sarge you want to go a round."

"Maizzie cut out the shit, how do you know this guy? he just scammed some old lady out of over a million dollars and you get a lousy thousand and here you are sitting in an interrogation room freezing your titties off. Give me something I can use and I'll personally cover your shoulders with my coat or maybe I should turn up the heat or my coat, which is it?"

Maizzie, "Why don't you go screw, I already told you all I know. What can you do to me? If they knew I blabbed they would slit my throat.So either let me go or charge me with something, I want a lawyer now." "OK Mazzie, we'll let you go but stay around town I don't want to have to come looking for you because then I will charge you as an accomplice and throw the book at you."

"You frigging cops are all the same it's hell trying to make a living in this town a girl like me should be living on easy street, any a reward??"

He just looked at her thinking, "I knew she was looking for an angle, after all the bluster she's looking for money these people have no conscience she would probably sell her first born for the right price." Mazzie, "come on let me see the green before I squeal on those two". "Yes, there is a reward of ten thousand dollars to anyone who can finger Jimmy K. and his partner Henry if you can do that I will make sure you receive the reward, so what do you know?"

"The only thing I know is I overheard them talking about their next scam was in Houston. He was going over the plan with that little Troll Henry. That guy creeped me out he has some weird ideas about how to please a woman. I just happened to look over his shoulder one night when he was on the computer when they were staying with me. He runs a scam telling women about how he is never loved and goes by the name "Henry". I guess the broads fall for the lonely line and the picture he shows on the internet is not him by a long shot." Sergeant Logan, "So what does he do so he can't be traced, do you have any idea?". "I think he uses something called a "BOT" don't really know computers are not my thing. He may look like a Troll but he sure can make a computer sing. The women love it he gets five or six hits a night. I heard Jimmy telling him to keep it in his pants till after the scam in Houston. That's all I know honest. I'm not sure but I think they are part of a bigger ring of thieves these scams are only part of what they are up too. I just overheard that there are other things going on, what they are I have no clue but all the money is hidden in a bank on the islands. You can't put this out on the street or I will disappear and end up floating in the river, please don't use my name. OH, one more thing they talked about some guy in California who scared them shitless, I think his name was Carl didn't get his last name."

"You can go now we will keep this under wraps when we want to talk to you we know where to find you. Appreciate the information."

The two detectives put their heads together the next hit would be in Houston they had to get a step ahead of those two, they to have accomplices all over the country.

So her story of a larger picture seemed to be correct it sounds like California is the main base and who is this Carl character, Who is feeding them personal information on their bank accounts? I have a memo from my office that Marjorie Swift is in FBI custody. A bunch of hired killers followed her to Canada and tried to snuff her out. "Wait a minute the guy she tried to kill in LA was Carl she supposedly skimmed some of the take and he tried to get rid of her. We questioned her and she disappeared. This James K. and Henry originally worked the LA area and are now headed to Houston there has to be a common link somewhere to tie all these people together."

CHAPTER: TWENTY EIGHT

"I just received the go ahead to partner with you we are to hunt Jimmy K. and Henry down no matter how long it takes." Lieutenant Morrison, "Before we do anything we have to find out who is on the board of directors of the banks our victims had money in. Think about it how do these two know who to pick as their targets, what their savings are, how vulnerable are they? they must have inside information."

The next morning the two detectives sat down and started to look at the board of directors and the employees of the banks that the victims had their savings in looking for a someone who could have information on all the people that had been scammed.

They placed all the names on the evidence board and only one name showed up as a member of the board, "Our friend Morty it has to be him what the hell is he doing on the board of a bank in Chicago? That hack is Carl's lawyer. Didn't Maizzie say that those two were scared of someone named Carl? This is all beginning to make sense. I'll bet if we can trace the phone number back to California it will led us to either Carl or Morty."

Morrison, "I called LA last night and checked out a couple of fancy country clubs and guess who is the owner of one of the wealthiest clubs in the LA basin?". "Let me guess Carl." "You got it brother these bastards are set up all over the country. The Police would never connect these crimes, they would stand alone, maybe that's why Marjorie Swift is being held by the FBI. There is definitely more going on than meets the eye."

Lieutenant Morrison's phone rang, "Hello what's that you say, where is she now? we'll meet you at the hospital." Sergeant Logan, "What's up?"

"They found Mazzie beaten and left for dead she's at the downtown Medical Center."

"I'll be a son of a bitch how did they know she talked? we must have a mole in the department, somebody is selling the Mob our Intelligence."

They drove to the hospital and went to her hospital room.

"We are looking for a Maizzie Smith what room is she in?"

Nurse "She's in room number six on the second floor. She still may be unconscious she was beaten pretty badly."

They entered the room she was barely conscious, "I told you if they find out I talked they would try to kill me. Get out of the room you two can go screw yourselves."

"Look Maizzie I'm sorry you need to tell us who did this." She started to scream, "Nurse, Nurse get these assholes out of my room now. I don't want them near me…HELP…HELP they are trying to hurt me", "OK, OK Maizzie we are leaving". "Jesus, she is pissed."

The nurse opened the door to her room, "Gentlemen you must leave now or I will call security". "We are leaving and we are both

Police Officers we have to question her she may be in danger. Someone definitely tried to kill her."

Lieutenant Morrison, "There is a problem in your Precinct I don't know who the snitch is but our only witness is in the hospital and I would bet when she is discharged they will finish the job."

Sergeant Logan, "Somehow we have to lay a trap and get the bastard to take the bait."

Morrison "Think about who in the office knows everything that transpires, is able to open files, can come and go as they please."

"I say we set up Shirley the secretary we tell her that Maizzie is in the hospital and so pissed she is going to tell us everything she knows. We move Maizzie give Shirley the old room number and see what happens."

Morrison, "I'll head to the hospital and set up everything, send one of the Patrol Officers to back me just in case". "I'll write up the report and ask her to file it and we'll see what happens."

When Morrison arrived at the hospital he had a couple of interns move Maizzie to another room, "I would appreciate it if you could stay with her till my backup arrives". "No problem she's sedated." He called Logan, "When will my backup be here?"

"He should be on site in thirty minutes, names Greg". "OK, sounds good." Morrison placed the phone in his pocket he had a strange feeling something was wrong, but couldn't put his finger on it.

He was walking to Maizzies old room when he spotted a uniform walking up the hall,"Great now we are all set, hey are you Greg?". "Yea, Logan sent me to give you a hand, where is she I'll guard her?". "I think we should occupy her old room and ambush the attacker."

As Morrison was talking he (had always been a stickler that any officers who worked with him that their uniforms be up to snuff). "What am I looking at?" he is wearing dress shoes and that side arm is a Kimber semi-automatic, "SHIT" he is a ringer a regular Officer couldn't afford a Kimber they go for over a thousand big ones I have to be cool or I am a dead man, "Sounds good to me let's check her room and then we can set up security." Morrison has a queasy feeling that the Hit Man is trying to figure out if he should make his move now or wait till they are alone in the room. If he screws up it will be a blood bath no one on this floor is armed. Morrison, "Yea lets check out her room and I will show you where I put her for safe keeping. She's not on this floor", he stepped aside to allow the hit man to enter the room and pulled his pistol, "Put your hands up and don't move or your a dead man", "What in the hell are you talking about Logan sent me over from Station". "If your legit hand over your weapon and I'll check you out."

He slowly unholstered his weapon and as he dropped it to the floor turned suddenly, Morrison saw the flash of a knife as the assassin plunged it into Morrison's chest, who was wearing a bullet proof vest, the knife went through the vest and struck his police badge underneath. The attacker struck with so much force that it drove Morrison to his knees and knocked the breath out of him. "You Son of a Bitch", his training came into play and as he was falling drew his gun and fired point blank at his attacker, he put three shots center mass. The assailant gasped and fell backwards, Morrison was about to holster his gun when he noticed the man he just shot was not bleeding, before he could act Morrison struck him with the butt of his pistol rolled him over and cuffed him.

He went through the hired killers pockets, frisked him for more weapons found a leg gun, a sap, and another Seal knife.

Sergeant Logan and two Officers slowly pushed open the door guns at the ready, "Holy Shit Jake, what happened are you alright?" Morrison stood up and turned around, "Damned Morrison you have a knife sticking out of your chest, I think you should sit down and I'll get a doctor in here to check you out," Jake Morrison was feeling weak he could feel something warm slowly running down his pants leg, looking at his shoe it was covered in his blood, "OH Shit" and thats the last thing he remembered as he collapsed on the floor.

Logan, "We need a Doctor in here now I have an Officer down." They rolled Morrison into an operating room the nurses slowly peeled back his bullet proof vest and his shirt.

"It appears the knife has driven his badge into his chest we have to make sure that it hasn't cut an artery." The Doctor sewed him up, "He should stay in the Hospital for a couple of days just in case the Lieutenant has complications."

Two days later Morrison was back in the station, "Who in the hell called in a Hit Man to kill Maizzie, what happened when you gave that report to Shirley. I no sooner moved Maizzie to safety than this bozo shows up dressed like a Police Officer. I spotted him right off he was wearing dress shoes and was sporting a Kimber semi-automatic worth at least twelve hundred or better, by the way did he talk?". "Nope couldn't get him to flip, he has no finger prints, or identification.Just asked for a lawyer."

Logan, "It can't be Shirley I hadn't even given her the memo and our boy shows up at the hospital I think the Station is bugged. I don't know who runs the operation but they are willing to kill anyone who talks."

Morrison, "Where's the shooter?". "The FBI has him and from what I could pry out of the Agents they are questioning Marjorie Swift about the operation also. I think there is White Slavery and Drugs involved on an International Scale."

"Just got word the FBI wants to question Maizzie we have a meet to turn her over to them at midnight" Morrison, "Who else knows about this? I say we go prepared bullet proof vests a couple of UZIES and plenty of clips. We are being watched I feel it in my bones."

Logan, "Keep cool, this is legit I talked to the lead Agent they want to keep her at a safe house along with Marjorie Swift."

When the two Detectives were outfitted they drove to the hospital and had the Doctor sign a release.

"Come on Maizzie the FEDs want to question you, we're taking you to a safe house and they will transport you to California."

Maizzie, "You two are total "Dick Wads" I wouldn't be surprised that this is a setup. I might sell it for a living but nothing would surprise me, Number One, I no sooner get settled in this jerky hospital and some gorilla shows up and tries to waste me, Number Two, you Schmucks have a leak in the Police Department as big as the Grand Canyon and you want me to believe I'll be safe, bullshit!!"

Morrison looks at Logan, "So what do you think?". "I say she has a good point this may be an ambush. We should have a couple of squad cars positioned near the trade off just in case she is right." They were almost to the meeting, "This is sure an out of the way to leave our package. I'm going to have one of our cars check things out before we move any further. Jake drive around and park in front of the SUV be careful and check it out to make sure it's not a setup",

"Got you boss, there doesn't appear to be any movement in the SUV it could be a bomb."

Maizzie, "For Christ sake get me out of here I told you this was a set up." Logan spots headlights in the rear view mirror. "Morrison we have company, Jake get the hell away from that SUV we are coming your way there is a bogey to our rear I think they are trying to box us in so when they set off the bomb it will take all of us out."

CHAPTER: TWENTY NINE

Logan backed up smashing the front of the car trying to keep them from escaping, there was a loud crunch and the driver exited the auto pulled an automatic and started to fire on them. The first shot shattered the rear window of the car Jones stepped on the gas and with the tires burning rubber left the attacker in a cloud of dust and stones.

"Maizzie get down!" Morrison fired through the rear window he emptied his Glock 18 and jammed another clip in firing at will with the second volley he heard a scream of pain and the attacker was seen holding his chest, blood dripping from his lips collapsed on the ground there was a momentary silence and the gunman in the passenger seat jumped out of the car and started firing. Luckily one of the Squad cars had circled back and Officer Mc Clark had loaded his shot gun and as they swung by the shooter fired twice the first blast removed his right hand and as he turned to return fire with his left Mc Clark blew away the left side of his head exposing his brain the shooter straightened up looking as if he was a zombie and fell flat on his face crushing his nose into the blacktop.

Mc Clark, "Wow, I think he just had a bad fall and crushed his face and he may need a brain transplant!"

Morrison, "Those two have been neutralized I say we get the hell out of here and bring in the bomb squad if that is an FBI SUV the occupants are either dead or dying." His cell started ringing,"Morrison this is Agent Josh Williams where in the hell are you we were supposed to meet at the Court House at ten tonight to pick up your ward Maizzie". "Who are you? I need more info before I turn over anyone to you we just escaped from an ambush I will meet with you at the Police Station in the morning after I check out your credentials."

"Look Morrison, this is bullshit I want her now or you are in deep shit", "See you in the morning", and he hung up.The FBI Agent was raving that bastard hung up", "Cool it Josh, we will see him in the morning something went real wrong tonight so you can't really blame him." Logan, "What did the Bomb Squad find?". "The SUV was set to blow they figure the blast would be caused by a burn phone. It was a definite set up the explosion would have taken out the entire crew. The car was loaded with enough C4 to destroy the whole block". "Logan I say we keep Maizzie at the Station tonight I'll take the first watch and why don't you take the second". "God Morrison don't you ever let up". "Not when I have the smell of blood we have them on the run. I'm going to squeeze till they make a mistake and then I will have the bastards." The next morning at eight sharp FBI Agent Josh Williams and his side kick arrived at the station. "Can you tell Sergeant Logan FBI Agent Josh Williams is here to pick up Maizzie Smith", "Hello Sergeant Logan, there is an FBI Agent here to pickup". "Just send him up, thank you."

They shook hands, "May I see your identification Josh we have a mole in the department and somehow they were able to lead us into a trap, we never received your instructions. The message we received almost got us killed. I need to guarantee that you are who you say you are."

Logan checked their finger prints, facial recognition and DNA, "Are you satisfied now? Sergeant Logan."

"Just one question why are you keeping two major witnesses at one Safe House? That could be a problem Morrison tells me that Marjorie Swift can be one hell of a handful."

"We can handle her the California office is geared to take on hard cases like Marjorie Swift. She is our main witness against Carl,she can connect him to Morty and the two missing scammers." "And what about Maizzie do you think you can wring any more intel from her brain? She's a good kid but I don't know how much she really knows."

"Are we done here? we will meet you in the parking garage second level". "Look Josh, are you sure you don't at least want us to give you backup to the airport. I am telling you these people will do almost anything to silence Maizzie, the reach of the this gang is world wide."

FBI Agent Josh Williams, "Look Sergeant Logan and your partner Lieutenant Morrison want to help, but the FBI can handle this Crime Syndicate or what ever you want to call it. Like I said, "We'll meet you in the parking garage to hand over the witness."

"Alright, have it your way we'll have her there in an hour, I wish you luck you will need it.

"Officer bring Maizzie to my office I need to advise her of her rights. The FBI has already signed that they take all responsibility for the witness."

Logan was sitting at his desk when Maizzie was being ushered into his office, "What the Frigging do you think you are doing first you almost get me killed and now you turn me over to some green FBI Agent. Carl's people will chew him up and spit him out and all the while I'm a corpse."

"Look Maizzie we have no choice they have jurisdiction this is a Federal crime", Her eyes started to water, "I don't feel good about this, Jesus can't you and Morrison tail us till we board the plane. I'm begging you Please, Please I know they are going to take us out, I don't want to die!!"

"Ok, Ok we will have you back up all the way to you boarding the plane, how's that". "Logan I could kiss you". "That's Ok, just keep this to yourself." He calls Morrison, "Lets go brother we have a job to do I promised Maizzie we would give them protection till they boarded the plane", "Logan you are as soft as they come", "Come on Morrison you got to give her an "A" for moxie."

They talked the FBI into letting the local Police give them extra protection to the airport. One Police Cruiser took the lead Morrison and Jones followed in the rear.

"I think we will be at our most vulnerable when we leave the station the street is narrow and wall to wall with three story brick homes" Morrison, "I say we send a Recon Team and a couple of snipers to check out the roofs before we start."

"Logan, I need you to stay behind and monitor communications, I'll take Jones to be my backup."

CHAPTER: THIRTY

The Recon Team fanned out and split up taking the roofs and some stayed on the street looking for any movement in the houses. "Jack it appears to be all clear but I still have a queasy feeling that something isn't right. There are no lights on in any of the buildings I know these houses are occupied but the place is like a tomb. Do you want us to start going from house to house knocking on doors?"

"Keep the snipers on the roofs and check out every other home." Sergeant, "We are half way down the block, the houses appear to be empty." Jack, "I'm telling you there is definitely something up, I just wonder if they are going to try to take you out with RPG's. They will eat up the half track and the FBI's armored SUV." Morrison, "Josh are there any satellites in the area that the FBI can use to scan these buildings for heat sources?"

"I'll call Washington and see what I can do, I agree this is definitely a weird situation. If I can't commandeer a satellite maybe the air base has a DRONE available that's able to read body heat in buildings". "Damned I feel like we're back in Iraq and the enemy is trying to suck us into a box with no way out." Just then Morrison half way down the block caught a flash of light reflected in a window on the second floor of one of the houses. Morrison, "Jack tell Mike to send a Tactical Team to the sixth house on the left, second floor I just caught a reflection in the window someone is up there". "Did you get that Mike?" "Roger that". "Be careful it may be a setup the place could be booby trapped". "Will use extremecaution, over and out."

Everyone sat back holding their breath. The Team took out the door and stormed the house. The team at the rear of the building stayed in place waiting for orders. All of a sudden there was automatic fire, a Flash Bang and then a grenade exploded the entire window frame blew out of the building and a body followed holding an RPG that miss fired and penetrated the brick wall of the house across the street everything seemed to happen in slow motion "SILENCE" then the blast wave from the explosion cracked the bullet proof glass on the armored cars causing everyone to duck as the wall was turned into a pile of dust, the entire front of the building to evaporate with a loud ear piercing screech. Morrison looked at Jack sitting next to him and he looked as if he had been sucker punched his nose was bleeding and blood was running out his right ear the pressure from the blast wave had blown his ear drum.

"Jesus, Jack are you alright? you are covered in blood." He just looked over at Morrison still in a daze, "What the Fuck just happened. That RPG must have had an Atomic war head. I have never seen anything like it. "Josh," We have eyes on the target the Air Force has an armed drone overhead the Controller is searching all the buildings as we speak for anymore signs of hostiles. Morrison, "Don't drop any ordinance on civilians, for Christ Sake Josh the News Papers will have a field day if they catch wind we bombed a neighborhood in the USA, have it checked for heat sources then back it off", "GEE, Morrison don't get your shorts all tight. So far there doesn't appear to be any more hostiles in the neighborhood." Jack, "Mike what in the hell just happened, Mike can you hear me do you have any casualties?". "Two men wounded that bastard was taking aim at the front vehicle what ever was loaded into that warhead was sure to take out the entire convoy. There were three hostiles in the room I took a chance and threw in a grenade to eliminate the danger of them being able to fire the RPG they just opened on us we retaliated with deadly force. We wanted to take a few prisoners, only trouble is they are all dead and I mean little pieces dead."

Jack, "No problem we'll get their DNA and run it through our data base I am sure we will be able to identify at least one of them" Josh, "Plans are changed they are flying in a Chinook CH-53K to take passengers and a AH-64 Apache helicopter as backup the White House is trying to figure out if this has International overtones the President is totally pissed."

Every one in the convoy is being flown to the Naval Hospital in Camp Pendleton to be checked out the pressure from the explosion could have caused internal damage. "Our Clean up Team is monitoring for Radiation before we send in our people."

The tow truck had just gotten the wrecked vehicles moved out of the way when the Copters arrived hovering. The parking lot was large enough to allow the Chinook to land and pick up passengers, the AH-64 held point overhead just in case there were anymore hostiles in the area. The loading took all of twenty minutes. As they were taking off Morrison saw at least a Company of Marines breaking down doors and searching every building on the street, "Damned, I wouldn't want to be whoever staged this little show their "ASS IS GRASS.""

When they deplaned from the Chinook at three in the morning medical Personnel escorted the patients into the hospital and had them put on hospital gowns. Every one was given brain scans, chest x rays and complete physicals. It was sunrise when the team had been completely checked out.

Looking out a hospital window Jack watched as a Limousine pulled up to the front of the building and a Three Star General exited asked to see Morrison, Jack and the FBI Agent Josh. They were to appear before the Security Council this morning for a debriefing. The President had declared DEFCON 4.

CHAPTER: THIRTY ONE

efore they were allowed to leave the hospital everyone signed a Classified Information Nondisclosure Agreement Form-312. "Gentlemen what you will learn at the meeting of the Security Council will be kept Top Secret and any disclosure could put you in Leavenworth for a period of ten years, do you understand??". "YES SIR","There is an armored carrier waiting for you downstairs the President is waiting."

On the drive to the White House there was complete silence.

The Carrier pulled around the rear of the White House and parked General Samules, "Time to exit their waiting for us in The Woodshed", Morrison, "What the hell is the Woodshed". "It's a acronym for the Situation Room", Jack answered, "There must be something going on we aren't aware of, I have a feeling that we will know very soon."

At the entrance to the Situation Room everyone was stopped and there was a container passed around, "Everyone please place their phones, weapons and any keys, or objects that will set off the alarm in the container, when you enter please take seats on the right of the President." Morrison glanced around the room there was the Head of the CIA, FBI,Homeland Security, any one with the need to know. The President, "Gentlemen we are here because the of the Enemies attack on our people on American soil with a Nuclear Tipped weapon. When our Ordinance Crew sifted through the debris of the explosion there were traces of Radiation. I'll let Colonel Jerome give the debriefing, he is in charge of our Nuclear Control program, When my people searched the site they found that the RPG that caused the explosion had been impregnated with remnants of spent Nuclear Fuel, we traced it to spent fuel rods in North Korea. I say we have a major problem whoever these people are they need to be taken out with Extreme Prejudice." The Chief of Staff, "As you are aware our friends in Pakistan have been selling Nuclear Technology to our enemies in the North. I say we read Lieutenant Morrison, Sergeant Jones and FBI Agent Josh in to our planning. Morrison and Jones will continue to pursue Jimmy K. and Henry, we feel that they have enough information to lead us to the ring leaders. They will work directly with the CIA and Homeland Security, Agent Josh will stay with the FBI he will have top Security Clearance and work in unison with all of our Departments."

"Morrison and Jones will fly to LA tonight to question Marjorie Swift believe it or not she was a Black OP who everyone thought was dead and what the hell ends up working for these scum bums. I am sure she knows much more than she is letting on." After they boarded the plane to LA Morrison and Jones started trying to put all the pieces together, "I have been working on this case for over a year and every day it gets more convoluted. Now we have some Foreign Mercenaries involved with Nuclear tipped weapons, it appears Carl is an underboss, I have a feeling this entire enterprise originates in China or Russia."

Jones, "From what you said there seems to be some collusion between City Hall,Police Department and the Hollywood Crowd. His Lawyer Morty put a lid on that Mogul being stabbed, as far as they were concerned it never happened."

Mysteriously the mansion burns to the ground and all the evidence goes up in smoke, Our Miss Swift disappears into the wilds of Canada and reappears with the FBI holding her in a safe house in California. Then our boy Benny the only Mercenary not killed or captured is God knows where. James K. and Henry have eluded the the authorities so far, they have never show up in Houston, Texas or anywhere else for that matter, where in the hell is everyone?"When they landed at the airport Morrison's cell phone began to ring, "Morrison this is Captain Sullivan I have been given orders by the CIA that you have cart blanche to do as you see fit and anything you need by way of help just ask" "Thank you Captain I will keep that in mind." He had a second call from the head of the FBI Bureau in LA, "Hello, who is this?"

Joe Cardilio "I run the FBI office in LA, I want to meet with you tomorrow morning and you can read me in on your assignment." Morrison "Pardon! I don't think so, you will have to contact Homeland Security or the CIA. Really you don't have a need to know. Our operation will be Top Secret."

"Look Morrison don't give me bullshit, I said meet me in my office and read me in."

He looks at the phone answering, "LATER, much later", and hung up.

Jones "Who in the hell was that?"

"Your boy that runs the LA office, wanted me to read him in to our operation."

"Joe Cardillo? knowing him he is probably all pissed off that he hasn't been given the lead in the investigation. Just watch out he will try to find out more than he needs to know so he can claim kudos, he's a real ladder climber."

Morrison, "I hear you, we stay away from him, big time." Marjorie was sitting next to Morrison listening to the conversation thinking "I can feel the tension between those two, they will probably take down half of Los Angelis to prove which one is the best man standing. This will be a real show when we are investigating the link between Carl and the foreign connection. Men drive me nuts I can feel the testosterone in the air. They should be a circus act competing as strong men." Morrison, "Marjorie, we need to de-brief you, what in the Hell do you know that is worth sending a dozen Mercenaries and placing a million dollar bounty on your head?, as far as I can tell you set people up to rob their homes, and that crazy Benny is still out there trying to collect the bounty. Think, think Marjorie what in the hell do you know that you'r not telling us?"

"I've been racking my brain believe me, wait a minute I overheard a conversation that Morty was having with someone they had an Oriental accent and I questioned him as to what in the hell were you guys into?, he told me to mind my own business. They were talking about weapons, YES! That's it they were talking about bringing in illegally manufactured weapons and Fentanyl from China. The ships call was Red Rose it was supposed to dock in LA a week ago It may still be in port." Jones "I've been hearing that the (CPB)U.S. Customs and Border Protection is having a heck of a time intercepting illicit gun parts from Shenzhen, China. Of course the (CCP) Chinese Communist Party disclaims any connection to the gun running or will admit that they are Chinese manufactured."

Morrison "I'll call the Port Authority to see if the Red Rose is still in port and ask for a warrant to search the ship."

Jones "We may have trouble getting a warrant the Port is still owned by COSCO (CHINA OCEAN SHIPPING CO.) I will check to see if the port is considered foreign soil." "With this information we may have to call Homeland Security to pull some strings. The President doesn't look very kindly to the CCP controlling our largest port he's making them sell it."

Morrison was told the Red Rose was registered in Panama and that she was still in port getting repairs. He called the CIA to see if they had any Drones in the area when the Red Rose was still twelve miles out, he wondered if they had off loaded cargo prior to stopping in Los Angeles. A couple of hours later Morrison's cell rang It was the CIA, "Can't talk on your phone it has to be on an Encrypted Line meet me tomorrow morning at our Headquarters. We have an area that can be isolated so that all conversations are kept secret."

"What about Jones and Marjorie Swift?"

"Yes, they will be read in also, we are still looking into her background and are keeping her on a short leash." They all arrived at the CIA Headquarters in the morning.

"Look Marjorie they are reading you in but still have reservations about your loyalties, so be cool understand? I think you will be under house arrest till all this shit blows over."

"YEA, YEA! I hear you I just want to see that Carl and Morty put away for years and years." They were met entering the building it looked like any office structure. "Please empty your pockets and place everything in the container on the counter." Another Agent ran a wand over their personal possessions and waved them toward an elevator."Your personal items will be here whcn you are leaving."

When they exited the Elevator a CIA Agent ushered them into a anti-room. "Everyone will need to give their Fingerprints, Palm Prints, please read the literature out loud for the Voice Print and we will need an Ocular Print. When that is complete you will be asked to sign a Non Disclosure Agreement is that understood?" They answered in unison, "Yes, we understand." Marjorie will stay in the room Morrison and Jones please follow me they entered and were met by an CIA Agent, build like a tank, probably an ex-Seal. "Gentlemen sit, we have been following the Red Rose for weeks, and yes there is surveillance footage of cargo being off loaded out to sea on a small barge, we have been tracking it since they loaded the cargo on a truck. As you are aware the CCP is unloading illegal weapons on US soil by the thousands. We know the BCO (Beneficial Cargo Owner) is a Chinese Commercial Outfit in San Diego. Can't quite figure out if they just think all American's are stupid or they just don't give a damned." He handed Morrison and Jones encrypted phones. "Never use your regular cell phones when contacting this office. You two are to investigate this Carl and Morty characters it must look like a regular investigation. We will put pressure from above to allow you to do your job without any interference, any questions?"

"Where did the Nuclear Tipped RPG's originate from?" "We believe it is spent fuel and the fingerprint points to North Korea."

"So it sounds as if these people could be traitors or just deal in anything to make money and screw the USA. Which makes them worse than Traitors."

Morrison, "Where does that leave Marjorie?". "Right now we have to clarify she hasn't been turned. She was a Dark Op and her last assignment went South. Marjorie claims that one of our people sold them out and got her people killed, we are looking into that but in the meantime she will be helping you in the investigation of Carl and Morty, when that is wrapped up, the FBI will put her under house arrest."

Jones, "What's your take on Carl or Morty I'm trying to figure out who's actually running the show". "We believe Carl is the brains, Morty is just a mouthpiece but there is definitely an International Criminal Organization behind this entire scenario. Carl is the front man in the states we have traced about half a billion dollars to banks in the Islands. They appear to be involved in anything that is illegal. In order to put Carl in prison you need to capture Jimmy and Henry and get them to talk. That Jimmy could probably bust the case wide open. "Every one stood up and shook hands," Jones "Did he introduce himself or am I mistaken?" Morrison "Now that you mention it nobody introduced themselves, I guess thats why they call them "SPOOKS", they both laughed as they left the building, with Marjorie in tow.

CHAPTER: THIRTY TWO

hey drove to the Airport the FBI had rented a private jet to fly the trio to LA, that's where Jimmy and Henry were last spotted. Jones parked in front of the Private Lounge they exited the car and entered.

Morrison, "The place is empty I thought we were supposed to be met by a couple of Agents from the Bureau to accompany us on the plane for backup? I wonder what in the hell is going on? it almost looks like a set up." Morrison, "why don't you take Marjorie to the safe room while I check everything out." Morrison, "Where is it ?". "It is two doors down the Promenade. I used it the last time I was here, we have to move. Something isn't right I can smell it." When they reached the door he entered the code and the door opened immediately. "Thank GOD they didn't change the code or we would be in a real bind." Marjorie was hustled inside, "Maybe they were held up I'll call the office and check their ETA." He spoke to someone in the FBI office and dropped the phone looking around slowly, whispering to Morrison.

"They called in an hour ago that they had arrived and will be taking up defensive positions."

Morrison is about to close the Safe Room door when he heard the sound of gunfire. "I wonder if anyone needs backup?"

He opens the door a crack and spies a Police Office taking cover behind a large concrete pillar and spies a shooter crawling on his belly attempting to take him in the rear. He opens the door enough to take a shot at the shooter, takes aim and fires, taking the attacker in the back of the head his blood and brains paint the floor a bright red dropping his rifle. The Officer glances in Morrison's direction, he gives him the signal come on in he hollers, "I have your back."

Marjorie, "There is a jet sitting on the runway. I bet they are waiting in the plane to ambush us. The agents are either dead or put out of action."

When they were all safe in the room Jones pushed a button and a large screen lit up. Jones, "I need to talk to the head of our office immediately, we have been compromised and in danger of being killed, find out who in the Department knew what our plans were because the enemy knew when and what Airport, Plane and time we were leaving and the two Agents who were to back us up are either deceased or put out of commission."

Morrison, "Marjorie, do you have your vest on? we don't want to lose you. You still have to be de-briefed." "Gee Boys, thanks for thinking about me, all I'm worth is my testimony? Morrison you are unquestionably on my shit list. You are such a misogynistic moron you think all women are for is to be used in some way or other. I'm beginning to wonder why I agreed to give evidence at all and now you tell me some wacko is out to kill me for a million dollar reward."

They could hear the Intruders trying to breach the Safe Room door. Jones, "Good luck the door is six inches of armored steel the same as the Army uses on their tanks, and the walls have rebar and are filled with five thousand pound concrete, just hope they don't have any C4 with them."

There was silence and an explosion that rocked the room the door and walls held, "What in the hell was that?". "They attempted to take out the door, we had better move to the rear corner of the room just in case they blast a hole in the wall."

Jones's encrypted phone started to ring, "You are safe open the door there is a company of Army Rangers on site they have eliminated the danger, we have three of them in custody."

He looked at Morrison, "What do you think are we being played?" "Ask them to give the call sign, we can't stay here forever." "Who am I speaking to? and what is the call sign. Then we open up". "This is First Lieutenant Simpson of the 75th Ranger Regiment the call sign is "Alpha Romeo 998". We need to move people there may be more hostiles on the horizon."

The door slowly opened, there stood a dozen Army Rangers.

Lieutenant Simpson, "We have an armored vehicle to take you to a waiting Plane on the west side of the air strip. My men haven't finished checking out your original transportation for booby traps, we will probably destroy the plane just to be safe." They were hustled into the Armored Vehicle, "It's a twenty minute drive to your aircraft. You people must be VIP's the President personally called out the 75th Rangers to rescue you." Morrison, "Sorry our operation is "Top Secret" cannot comment." When they boarded the plane they were met by a Stewardess.

Marjorie noticed the curtains were drawn and the window blinds closed. Behind them sat six men. "What can I get everyone to drink?",

Morrison, "I'll have a double BURBON on the Rocks," Marjorie, "Martini dirty," Jones, "A Club Soda."

As the jet taxied for takeoff one of the guards in the rear of the plane walked forward and tapped Morrison on the shoulder, he looked up and standing there was one tall and extremely muscular dude, he was all muscle, six four, crew cut and no one to screw with. Morrison, "Can I help you?"

"Names, Charley Tillison my men and I have been given the pleasure of being your protection till you put these guys in the Federal Pen." Morrison, "Have you been read in to our mission?" "Yes sir, They haven't given me all the details, my CO. said it would be up to you to fill in the details,I know that we have some hostiles running around with Nuclear Tipped weapons. They need to be taken out with Extreme Prejudice."

While they were still in the air Morrison's encrypted phone rang,"Hello". "Don't say anything, just listen. There is a Sergeant Petroff on board we picked up a signal from his phone that was traced to the Russian Embassy. Then the Embassy sent a coded message to a CCP Destroyer, the message was"It is imperative that you take them out before they land in LA, if you must sacrifice you life for the cause so be it."

Morrison taps Charley Tillison on the shoulder, "We have a problem, do you have a Sergeant Petrfoff under your command?" "Hell yes, he is one of my best men". "Is he armed?" Tillison, "We all are", "You need to neutralize him immediately", "He's a Mole the CIA has information that he has been given orders to take the plane down, now! at the cost of his own life."

Lieutenant Tillison turns without answering and walks to the rear of the plane, he reaches into his coat pocket and slowly removes a garrote holds it in the palm of his hand. He walks behind Sergeant Petrfoff and motions for the Agent sitting in the seat behind his target to give up his seat. As soon as the seat is vacant Lieutenant Tillison moves into the space and with lighting speed has the garrote around Sergeant Petrfoff neck. He orders Staff Sergeant Adams, "Grab his arms don't let him move he is wearing an Explosive Vest with a dead man switch."

He pulls the garrote tighter, and there is a groan as it cuts into the flesh around the neck and blood slowly trickles onto his shirt. Petrfoff is struggling attempting to remove his hold on the Dead Man Switch and complete his mission, Adams pulls off his belt, wrapping it around Petrfoff's hand. With his free hand Tillison throws him a roll of tape,"Make sure he can't let go of the switch, you don't just stand there open the emergency door, the door opens, "Pick the Traitor's Ass up and throw him out of the "Fucking Plane" before we are all blown to smithereens." Two Agents pick up the half dead Traitor and heave him out of the emergency door and close it. A few seconds pass and there is a bright flash, "What in the Hell was that?", "He probably thought it would be less painful than meeting the blacktop at a hundred miles an hour, so he committed suicide."

CHAPTER: THIRTY THREE

Tillison walks to first class, Morrison has just finished his BURBON Neat. "How did it go?". "Your Intelligence was correct, the Bastard was wearing a vest loaded with C4, he had to be working with the Russians" Morrison, "And probably the CCP they have placed spies in every Western Country on Earth."

"I have Petroff's burn phone, I'll have my people track the phone numbers. Our ETA is twenty minutes, we are landing on a secret airstrip on the outskirts of the city."

The plane circled the airstrip and finally landed. There were three Armored SUV's waiting for them.

Morrison, "Jones, Carl's mansion needs to be sealed off,Marjorie you go with Jones and show him where you think the bodies are buried. The FBI has agreed to work with the local Police Department and supply any equipment necessary to locate the missing family members, their loved ones and parents need closure". "This is Agent Jones I want you to send a crew to Carl's burnt down mansion. The entire area should be cordoned off no reporters allowed until I say so, I'll have the FBI meet you there with the Ground Radar. My "ETA" at the site in one hour." Morrison pulls Lieutenant Tillison aside, "Take a couple of your men and shadow Marty he's Carl's lawyer I believe he's into this up to his neck, also check the hospital to see how our boy Carl is doing."

On the drive to the Mansion Marjorie started to talk, "I was approached by Marty asking if I wanted to make some money by setting rich men up and robbing them. I said I didn't want anything to do with blackmail, he assured me all I had to do was weasel their safe combinations and alarm codes he had people that would take care of the rest. That's where I met Jimmy K. and Henry. Jimmy was the second story man Henry was his backup. Little did I know that Marty had set me up with him so they could keep track of the take. I was in on the orgies at the mansion that mysteriously burned down. Those parties had every drug you could think of. I know some of the women disappeared and I wouldn't be surprised if they were buried in the basement. The Party goers were mucky mucks from city hall, a bunch of Hollywood types and a few Cops I guess you get my drift. They were into selling hot cars overseas, dealing in drugs, white slavery, and on and on anything to make money. Oh Yea, at one of the parties there were people from the Chinese and Russian Embassies, as for Jimmy and Henry the last I heard they were headed for Houston."

When they pulled up to the site the crew had already taped off the property. From what you are telling me it appears we have an International Crime Syndicate on our hands."

Jones phone rang, "What's up Morrison?", "We just picked up intel that they are going to try to attack the crew at the Mansion and destroy evidence. I recommend every one on the site wear bullet proof gear and be armed, set up snipers around the premises in two man teams, don't take any chances."

Jones called to the Agent in charge, "Charley pass out Bullet proof vests and make sure everyone is armed there is Intel that we are expecting unwelcome visitors."

Marjorie, couldn't keep quiet any longer, "Where's my protection I wouldn't trust you to protect a fire hydrant, I took out six of those big boys in the Canadian woods, shit I could probably take you and a couple of others down too, what do you say do I get a piece or not?"

"NO! you do not get a piece I would loose my job if I gave you a weapon. I'll bet when you were younger you never married and if you were you probably scared the pants off of the poor bastard, so please let me do my job."

"Sergeant see if the City can close off the street, take a couple of men and move the Press away from the building if we are attacked I don't want any civilians wounded or killed."

He climbed into the Forensic Van and used it to block the main entrance. The Reporters were refusing to move, Jones could hear them shouting questions, taking pictures hoping someone would clue them in as to what was going on, but so far the Agents were ignoring them. After about an hour Jones let out a sigh, "I guess I better give the Press some kind of story or they will make up one of their own. But what the hell they do that anyway, if they don't like what they hear they'll just make up a story."

Jones walked to the entrance and held up his hands for silence. "This is what I can tell you at the present time, we believe that bodies may be buried on the property, we are using Imaging Equipment to ascertain if there are any bodies buried on the site". "Do you know who owns the Mansion?". "No, we haven't been able at this time to track down the owner". "How many bodies are buried here?" Marjorie, "As I said there may not be any bodies buried here and no I don't know who the killers are, come on people you know I can't give out that information this is an ongoing investigation. That's all for now if we find anything I will personally let you know so please step off the property and let my men do their job, thank you!". "Hey boss, I think we have something positive, there appears to be more than one body could be three or four". "Hey Frank take over the machine and I'll get a laborer to jack hammer this area be careful just breakup the concrete we don't want to destroy evidence or disturb the body." Everyone stood around while the laborers carefully removed the broken concrete. The Forensic team had donned their gear and carefully started to brush the debris from the bones.

"It definitely appears to be a young woman. I won't be able to tell how she died till I have her on a slab and do an autopsy." Jones, "Alright clear all the debris on the slab and lay out a six foot by six foot grid. There could be a dozen more bodies buried under the concrete." They gridded the slab and found twelve more bodies, It took the Forensic Team three days to remove the bodies and start transporting them to the morgue. "Any movement on the threat to close us down?". "No sir I think when they saw we had blocked the street with armored vehicles they had second thoughts". "Keep alert, I want you to take the armored SUV and back up the Ambulances they will be vulnerable to attack until you reach the morgue."

Jones took Marjorie aside, "How did you know about the bodies?" "I would go to bed with some of these slime balls and they would talk in their sleep or when they were drunk would brag about what went on at their meetings. They were into Devil worship I kind of thought it was all bullshit until a couple of prostitutes disappeared around the same time they were having the rituals. I stayed as far away from the mansion as possible till the night I was supposed to meet Carl Karlissone and the son of a bitch tried to strangle me and I stabbed the creep."

"Then what happened?". "The bum would have bled out if I hadn't called an ambulance. They thought I had become a liability and wanted me out of the way. Little did they know I was an ex-Army Ranger, had Black belts in Karate and Weapons, plus my military training that scum bag got a real surprise when I stuck him with my pig sticker." Jones took a step back he was impressed, Marjorie wasn't anyone to screw with, "So how in the hell did you get tangled up with this crew?". "They approached me and for a ten percent cut it was a worth my while, all I had to do was screw a few of these losers for a few thousand dollars to rolling in the hay with them knowing I had helped clean out the safes and they were clueless". "I will say one thing you tell it like it is, you sure don't pull any punches". "And about me being married, my husband was killed in an ambush in the Mid East he was also a Ranger and I couldn't take another loss like that so I stay at home and use a vibrator, it's safer that way. I have a teenage daughter in a private school far, far away from all this garbage." Jones just looked at her and started to laugh, thinking, "You never really know a person and she was a pip to say the least". "I have to give you credit, I guess if I was in your position I would have hidden in the Canadian woods also, because these boys would have snuffed you out if you had stayed in LA. Now you are working for the good guys."

CHAPTER: THIRTY FOUR

The Ambulances were positioned in the center of the motorcade Morrison stationed a Armored SUV in front and another in the rear, the President had allocated a company of SPECIAL FORCES dressed as civilians who were strategically located along the motorcades route, especially at cross streets and bottlenecks where the Maoists and criminal hostiles would be able to cut off and isolate the Ambulances while keeping the armored vehicles busy trying to defend themselves. The advanced team had eyes on a number of hostiles who appeared to be taking up positions where the main street narrowed to one lane for two city blocks.

The Captain in charge called Morrison for instructions, "Hey boss we have embedded hostiles a quarter mile from the convoy whose ETA is ten minutes need orders on how to proceed". "Is there any way to evacuate civilians?". "We can put lay down suppressing fire to keep them at bay till I send in some of my people to clear the structures, from the building plans I have they will be able to escape through the rear of the buildings, will send two Fire Teams around the rear of the buildings to keep the enemy at bay while we evacuate". "I say we declare them "DHF" a Declared Hostile Force, but all civilians are to be removed immediately."

Captain Donovan, "First Sergeant sent a Fire Team around the rear of the structures and use suppressing fire to contain the enemy till we clear the buildings of civilians. There are two Apaches on the way to box them in" First Sergeant, "I need two, four men Fire Teams now! they are to hold the rear of the buildings till we remove any civilians is that understood?" "Sergeant make sure each team is armed with M240L machines guns do not have them engage the enemy unless it is necessary." "Captain we have incoming enemy drones at approximately one thousand feet". "Lieutenant we have two Laser Guns that are capable of taking out Enemy Drones now is the time to see if they are as good as advertised". "Staff Sergeant we have an enemy drone on our screen, take the bastard down". "Yes Sir!"

The Laser was aimed at the incoming drone the beam invisible to the naked eye struck the drone dead center, the drone exploded with such a force that it disintegrated in midair. "Holy Shit, that thing was loaded with C4". "We picked up two more drones on our radar, we have two Laser Guns lets put an end to this shit". "We have them acquired. Fire at will."

They disappeared in a bright flash leaving nothing but black ash falling silently to the street. "Damn, I love these Laser Guns as the Sergeant kissed it," "Thank you Captain I'll follow you anywhere into battle."

"Captain the Fire Teams are in place". "have two men sweep the buildings for civilians and send them to the rear, they have ten minutes to complete the sweep before we make contact with the enemy". "Captain, Morrison is on the line," What can I do for you?".

"Just to let you know we have placed a two block perimeter around the fire zone and evacuated all the residents no one can get in "Tango" whatever hostiles are in your fire zone, take as many prisoners as possible we need to be able to figure out how deep this goes. As far as we can tell we haven't been able to detect any Nuclear material. The President has given an ultimatum to foreign powers suspected of using or selling to Americans' enemies can expect an immediate response.

"Sounds good to me, it's about time we had a President with a big pair of balls the last one was a real looser". "OK Boys, enough politics time to take on the enemy." The rest of the company fanned out across the street. "Captain, all the civilians have been evacuated and are out of the fire zone."

Just as he turned to give the order to advance there was the tat, tat sound of a machine gun, everyone hit the dirt.

Morrison, "Jones keep your people working on the site, I have a feeling there is more to be found here than bodies. I have commandeered two Helos to give you cover while you work."

"I don't believe this shit, we have a full blown fire fight in the middle of Los Angeles. These bastards need to be taken out and shot."

The team continued to scan the concrete slab, Jones had everyone wear bullet proof jackets and set up screens to give them cover from any snipers who may have broken through. He sent three two man sniper teams to the hill overlooking the house to control any fire by the enemy.

"Jones, we've found what looks like a safe buried in the cement. I'll bet this is what this is all about". "Maybe we hit the jackpot, it could hold all the information to bring down the entire operation."

Just then a bullet whizzed over their head and everyone was clawing at the concrete trying to climb into the open graves. Jones called the snipers "Are you assholes asleep we are being fired on", "Trying to get a bead on the bastard boss, There he is on the roof of one of the mansions across the street. I'll take him out but it looks like they have infiltrated the next block of houses."

Just as the enemy sniper was taking aim there was a loud "CRACK" and then silence. That's the last shot he'll ever take, you need to send a team to check out those two mansions across the street post haste, before they set up another nest."

Morrison looked across the road, there were two Black Hawk copters with Special Forces dressed in black repelling to the roof of the mansion. The first Special Forces on the roof set up a fire zone to protect their exposed comrades, enemy fighters scaling the mansions walls, were attempting to take out the Copters. Lieutenant, "Sergeant lay down fire on the edge of the roof, I'll direct the Black Hawks to take out the enemy on the ground gathering to assault the Special Forces." There was an immediate sound of gunfire, the Black Hawks opened up with their machine guns to give the troops backup and keep the enemy off balance.

CHAPTER: THIRTY FIVE

orrisons encrypted phone dinged and he received an E-Mail, "Enemy has been eliminated. Would recommend the convoy change route, have spotted hostiles beyond perimeter, over and out". "Sergeant, alert the convoy we are changing our route, have everyone turn left at the next street and take another left at the next corner. We will cover the rear of the convoy if I am correct the enemy has probably tapped into our communications, so scramble all messages from now on". "Yes sir will do."

The convoy turned left and Morrison noticed a pickup truck approaching the Armored HUMVEE.

"Sergeant man the machine gun, fire a warning round at that incoming pickup, if they ignore the warning take them out that truck is probably loaded with C4."

The Sergeant fired a a burst from the machine gun, the driver of the truck stepped on the gas and increased speed. Without hesitation the Sergeant opened fire with the M2 heavy machine gun that was loaded with armor piercing ammo, the first burst stopped the pickup dead in it's tracks the the second round of fire hit the C4 in the bed of the truck, this caused the truck to disappear in a bright flash followed by a vacuum and in a few seconds the entire block was rocked with a ear splitting explosion. The driver of the HUMVEE punched the gas petal hoping to be able to shelter them from the force of the blast just as the rear of the HUMVEE passes behind the corner of the building the Blast Wave catches the rear of the HUMVEE causing the back of the vehicle to careen to the left but the increased speed allowed the driver to bring it under control.

Morrison, "Don't slow down the corner building is liable to collapse from the explosion."

The words were no sooner out of his mouth than the front of the building collapsed into the street followed by a loud roar as the rest of the building walls imploded and the structure disappeared into a pile of dust. "Jesus boss, I sure hope nobody was home". "I have a message from the lead SUV, All clear our ETA to destination twenty minutes."

The convoy drove into the parking garage, and they began to unload the bodies. Morrison, "Adam how long will it take to figure out when the women died?". "Look Lieutenant, It will take me at least a week to Number one figure out how they died, and Number Two Identify the victims, the forensics will take at least thirty days". "Look Adam this case is High Priority, Homeland Security, CIA and the FBI are up my butt. Tell me what you need, I can have any number of Labs help with the Forensics, how about Pathologists, you can oversee the entire operation. Think man you will get all the kudos. When the operation is completed."

"Alright, Morrison I expect six experienced Pathologists by seven tomorrow morning and a list of Forensic Labs that will work twenty four hours a day to give me answers."

Morrison, "Done, done and done!!"

He was on the phone half the night calling in all the favors he could and then some. By midnight he had scrounged up four Pathologists and had three Labs promise to complete the Forensics within forty eight hours. At seven the next morning he called the Head Pathologist Adam, the phone rang twice and he picked up, "Adam it's Morrison I have been able to scrounge up four Pathologists who should be there within the hour and three local Labs that will work with you on the forensics."

"Sounds great, that will allow me to work on five victims at a time, hopefully by the end of the week I will be able to identify the victims and the cause of death."

Morrison, "Will check in later today to make sure everyone shows up, I won't bother you till the weekend but if you find anything you know how to get in touch with me."

Adam, "Will do, now let me get to work." Morrison arrived at the Mansion site, "Jones did you find any thing that would link Carl to the CCP or the North Koreans?". "I found a safe concealed in the floor, I had to bring in one of our safe crackers but this morning we finally cracked it. I didn't want to use any explosives because I was afraid any paper or fragile evidence would be damaged. The Army lent us a couple of their NCO's that spoke Korean, Russian and Chinese just in case we ran into a translation problem". "What about the Press?". "We have an Imbedded Journalist on site he is given a nightly report and any thing that is Secret will be redacted. We definitely don't want any information about Nuclear armaments getting out, you know these people if they don't know what's going on they will make up something out of thin air."

"Have you had any problem with Hostiles?". "Not since the Rangers occupied the Mansions across the street and placed snipers on the hill above the site, it has been quiet but I wouldn't be surprised if the bastards didn't try something in the next couple of days. Our overhead Satellite has spotted low flying drones attempting to encroach on our air space. We have a couple of Drone Busters, they screw up the enemies command and control functions causing them to crash land."

"Been able to track them back to their base?". "They keep moving their base every other day. We have some of our people scouting the area where the Drones are being launched from, so far they are only doing Recon if it gets nasty The Army Rangers will take them out." Captain Lee, "Sergeant Major how many Drone sites have your men located?". "Six Captain, I have sent teams to shut them all down if they refuse my people have orders to destroy the equipment and take everyone into custody."

CHAPTER: THIRTY SIX

orrison, "Jones, I want you to apply for two "No Knock" Federal Warrants there is a Federal Judge from the Ninth Circuit waiting for you so she can approved the warrants. We have to bring in Morty and Carl before they disappear, this is International it has crossed four State lines, the Canadian border, and has the smell of Russian and Chinese interference in the USA's sovereign affairs."

Jones, "I will call the Judge and tell her we need the No Knock Warrants because there is reason to believe that evidence will be destroyed if we give the people of interest time to react, we have to bring those two in for questioning, so far we have found around a dozen bodies and God knows how many other corpses are buried in the concrete slab not counting the Mansion grounds. This site is a grave yard without headstones."

His appointment with the Judge was at 2:45, she said that she would sign the Warrants only if the FBI promised to not use the warrant for anything other than what she had approved. "These people are both very rich and powerful don't give them any reason to slip out of your clutches, so do us all a favor and don't over reach".

"Yes, your honor I will do exactly as you ask." She handed the warrants to Jones, "Good luck!"

An hour later two Armored SUV"s pulled up to Morty's office. "Send six men around to the rear of the building and the rest of the crew follow me." He knocked once, then twice, "Kick the door in." Meanwhile Morty was at his desk working, "Who in the hell is knocking, I don't have time for this." Just as the words were uttered, there was a loud crashing sound, the glass in the door shattered, throwing shards across the office and the door screamed as it flew across the room taking the frame with it landing on the floor with a resounding crash.

Morty was startled as a half a dozen Agents dressed in battle gear stormed through the door. "Don't move keep your hands where we can see them place them on the desk, where do you keep your files?" Morty pointed to the file cabinets against the wall.

Agent, "Is this all of them?" Morty hesitated then pointed to the next office, "I keep my closed cases in the next space. What are you looking for? I would be glad to help you." He was ignored as the Agents took a battering ram and crashed through the door, "Call the office and tell them we need a box truck to handle all these files. They are stacked six feet deep and up to the ceiling."

One of the Agents hollered, "Boss, I think we hit the mother load."

"Take pictures of everything cabinets, boxes, furniture and log it in the manifest. I have to report back to the judge and give her the a list of what we have taken as evidence."

Morty started to gag, he was so upset that he began to vomit and went into a seizure, his eyes rolled back in his head and he slumped to the floor.

"Don't stand there give him oxygen I can't afford to have this slime ball die on me, make sure to clear the slime out of his throat, or he will suffocate on his own puke."

They rolled him over on his side and cleared his airway, then proceeded to administer oxygen, he started to come too. They sat him up, took his pulse making sure he wasn't having a heart attack. "He's coming around and his color is getting better."

"Take him downstairs and place him in the wagon and I want you two to stay with him all the way back to the office, if he dies it's on your asses."

"OH, by the way where is your partner Carl? he is next on our list the other team tells me he cannot be found where did he disappear to? if he's in LA we will find him make no mistake." Morty just kept shaking his head and shrugging his shoulders, "I have absolutely no idea where he is." When they arrived at the office Morty was placed in a holding cell, it had a single light bulb hanging from the ceiling. The heat had been turned up to ninety degrees and the cell smelled like stale urine. He screamed, "YOU CAN'T DO THIS TO ME, I didn't do anything I want to see a lawyer, this cell is an abomination no human should be treated like this, this cell stinks of human piss and why is it so hot in here? Please let me out I will tell you whatever you want to know please, please."

Morty broke down and started to cry, the Agents couldn't believe their ears," this guy broke before we even started to question him". "I'll bet he is looking to deal. He knows that once we start going through those files he is in a world of shit. I say we put him in the interrogation room, give him a cup of coffee and a donut. He will start to blabber and we probably won't be able to shut him up."

"OK, but no donuts that is carrying it to far he will have to suffer with a burger."

"Just put him in the room and keep your weird humor to yourself."

They moved Morty to the interrogation room, sat him in a chair and cuffed his left hand to the table in such a manner that he was placed in an uncomfortable posture pulling his body to one side. They left Morty sit alone for about an hour, then two Agents entered the room and just stood there and laid a pile of files on the table in front of him. One Agent sat down and across from him and the other Agent leaned against the wall.

Morty, "Hey Guys, please loosen the cuff so I can straighten up this position is killing my back, I'm an old man and this shit will put me in an early grave. I'll tell you everything I know, so please loosen the cuff."

The Agent walks over to Morty and loosens the cuff.

"OK, I'm listening it better be worth while or your butt will end up in solitary and your bunk will be the concrete floor, your lucky your an American citizen or your ass would be on the way to "GITMO.""

Morty stared at the Agent then turned his head slowly and gazed at the other Agent, the blood drained out of his face and placed his face on the table and started to laugh, "The stupid Son of a Bitch did it he helped the CCP sneak in Nuclear Tipped weapons. I warned him not to get mixed up with those people, it would be his downfall."

The Agent across the table sat straight up and the other Agent pulled up a chair and sat alongside of Morty. "Now where in the hell is Carl? I am tired of your bullshit". "Last I heard he was in Astan the capital city of Kazakhstan, the American government doesn't have an extradition treaty."

"What did you mean you warned him not to get involved with those people?"

"They are a breakaway group from the Chinese military that have gone Rogue and are partners with the North Koreans. They paid Carl millions to help them smuggle in Nuclear Tipped weapons. Even the CCP is having trouble controlling them, the feeling is that their true aim is to cause enough chaos in the States that it will tilt in their favor and at the same time they plan to take out the top people in the CCP and all the rest of the party will fall in line. This would give them control of the two most powerful countries on the planet."

CHAPTER: THIRTY SEVEN

"I don't believe a word you said, your trying to get us off track. Now how do we get to Carl? and don't give me anymore garbage about a Rogue Army, DO YOU HEAR ME?" Morty, "Like I said, he's in Kazakstan and they don't exactly like the USA but they love the American dollar. I would guess Carl spread a few million dollars so they would let him stay. He was tipped off as soon as the FBI started to seal off the Mansion and dig up the concrete". "You'r telling me we have a Mole in our operation?" Morty wiped the sweat from his forehead and he said, "Look that's all I know about the weapons. Carl mentioned it briefly and I said it was a bad idea." Agent, "So who is the mole Morty? I won't ask you again, I need an answer". "I don't know."

"What about all the corpses under the slab at the Mansion, I guess they are a big surprise also?"

"I never went to any of those parties they turned me off."

"So your saying you have no knowledge that there were women being murdered there, what exactly was going on? We are being told that there was devil worship and they were being sacrificed at the Mansion."

"That's all bullshit, I have never heard anything like that whoever told you that tale were lying through their teeth. Never happened, absolutely not I swear on my mother's grave."

"There you go trying to blow smoke again, if you want a deal we need the whole truth or your going up the creek for life. We have a witness as a matter a fact she is sitting in our office as we speak. She's a friend of yours, you know the friend you sent mercenaries to Canada to kill". "That's a lie." Agent, "I'm going to interrogate you and Marjorie at the same time, we'll see who is lying." The blood drained out of Morty's face and he became agitated with fear, he pissed his pants. "Please, don't put her in the same room with me she is one crazy bitch I heard what she did to the crew sent to take her out. Come on! you wouldn't leave her in here with me alone?". "So tell us what you do know Morty?". "Look guys I don't know anything about bodies, I can tell you about the car racket where we send cars overseas, I can tell you about the drugs, how we screwed old ladies out of their money, second story jobs, absolutely nothing about Nuclear Weapons or some women being murdered."

"Your sure that's all you know, we aren't going to find you are lying to us when we go through your files, you are sure??"

"I've told you all I know I need a deal and it has to be in writing and signed by the Federal Prosecutor and the head of the FBI or no deal. There probably is a price on my head as we speak so what do you say do we have an agreement or not?"

"Let me think about it, Bob lets go get a coffee and relax, we'll be back in a few minutes."

The two Agents sat in the cafeteria drinking their coffee. "Jesus Tom, what was all that crazy shit that Morty was spouting about a Rogue Chinese Military."

"Look Bob you are just on Probation this is way over your grade, you let me take care of it and don't let anyone know about it or the higher ups will probably can you. I am sure this is hush, hush you get my meaning? don't forget you answer to me."

Meanwhile Morty was getting nervous, "I need a deal or I am a dead man." Just then the door opened and the two Agents entered, "You have a deal, you know how this works if you hold back anything the deal is void and we could just put you out on the street and let the vultures circle to see who would collect the bounty. I'll bet there are a few of the boys who would love to see you in a coffin so they could take your place."

"Look, I told you I would tell you everything and I will, so write up the deal and get it signed and I will tell you where all the skeletons are buried."

Tom, "Bob you watch the prisoner and I will call my boss and the Federal Prosecutor so I can get the paper work started we need to move on this quickly before the rest of the ring have time to clean up their act or disappear like our friend Carl. I'll bet that fat bastard has blood on his hands and we still don't know who actually owns that Mansion."

Tom enters the Interrogation Room shaking his head, "They said they will think about giving you a deal there is too much at stake right now, so I'm going to have to let you go Morty I should have an answer in the morning."

Morty went nuts, "What the hell is going on I'm the only one who knows everything, what are your bosses thinking?"

"You can't do this to me I am a dead man." Tom didn't answer, he looked at Bob the other Agent, "Show Morty to his car, and walk away." Morty drove out of the parking garage trying to understand what just happened. He pulled onto the main highway and punched the gas petal he was pushing one hundred miles an hour when there was a bright flash and the last thing he knew the world ended for Morty. His Mercedes evaporated into a molten pile of plastic and metal. All they found at the site was his two SS tecth.

CHAPTER:
THIRTY EIGHT

ack at the Mansion site they had found six more bodies it appeared that there were four males and two females.

Morrison thinking, "This site apparently has been used as a dumping ground for years, I think I'll give Adam a call and see if he has been able to identify any of the remains."

"Adam what do you have for me it's been a week and we have uncovered six more remains, have you been able to identify anyone at the lab?"

"Yes, we have been able to get DNA samples from four and Dental records have identified three. It appears some of the women died from drug overdoses, four of the victims have either died from broken necks or blows to the skull. I will send you what I have, found one of the victims was a Lawyer who filed a law suit for sexual harassment against Carl, three were prostitutes. Working on the rest will keep you appraised."

Morrison walked over to Jones, "So what the scuttle butt on Morty and Carl?"

"You won't believe what happened, they had Morty in custody and from what I hear he was going to give up the goods and somehow his deal was put on hold. So they let him walk and twenty minutes later while he is driving on the highway his car disintegrates in an explosion killing Morty, so there goes our snitch."

Morrison, "I think we have a mole in the Bureau how did they know where he was and where he parked his car it was in a Federal Secure area. This shit is entirely out of hand."

Jones, "To change the subject at least we have an idea where Carl disappeared to Morty tagged him in Kazakhstan, the CIA is trying to see if the government will give him up. Last I heard Carl has bribed everyone from the President to the Mayor of the town where he is hiding, the scuttlebutt is he spread three million dollars around and the Government in Kazakhstan wants six million or they won't turn him over to us."

Morrison, "It's a stall I'll lay money on it they know we won't pay and they will never let the CIA operate in their country. It's just to give him time to escape and by the time they give in he will be long gone,God knows where."

"Lets get back to digging up the site I say we set up a working conference on Wednesday at twelve. I want everyone involved in this Investigation with evidence concerning this case I don't want to hear any bitching this is top priority, especially the Agent that handled Morty and his Aid." "Relax Morrison I will make sure everyone is there."

"Hello, Helen this is Jones I have a favor to ask Morrison wants you to set up a working conference for Wednesday at twelve concerning the Mansion site and make sure everyone involved is there and bring whatever evidence they have. Especially Tom and Bob we question why they allowed Morty to slip through the cracks". "Will do,I have everyone involved with this case on the roster. If I can't find anyone I will let you know". "Thanks I'm counting on you." Helen, "We're all set for Wednesday". "Sounds good, one of our four male victims was an undercover officer the department had written him off as an MIA, he was following up a lead on the Chinese Tong and drug dealing. Every thing leads back to Carl and Morty this Mansion must have been their main place of business. We have The Chinese Tong, drugs, smuggled weapons, prostitution, etc."

"What our main concern is Nuclear Tipped Weapons. Morty let slip that Carl was paid a few million dollars to help smuggle them into the country". "I still think if we can find Jimmy and Henry they will be able to give us much better insight as to this entire operation functions. After Wednesday's meeting I say we turn this operation over to one of our Forensic experts that will leave us free to track down those two scum bums." Morrison's phone rings, "Now what, hello who is this?, you want us to do what, and go where? yes sir I realize who I am speaking too." Jones, "Who in the hell was that?". "It was the Director of the CIA he has just ordered us to be on a plane to Kazakhstan tomorrow evening. They have a fix on Carl and the Kazakhstan's Prosecutor General has given permission for the us to return Carl to the United States, pack your bags." They arrived in Astana at eight in the morning Kazakhstan time hailed a cab and checked into the Hilton.

Jones, "We have a meeting with the authorities at noon they will give us the necessary papers so we can legally remove Carl from foreign soil, they said everything must be Hush, Hush because Carl has bribed so many people." Earlier that morning, bang, bang, "Who in the hell is banging on my door," "Carl wake up, God dam-it Carl answer the door". "I'm coming keep calm, sweetheart why don't you leave out the rear door I don't have a clue who is calling." He put on his bathrobe and opened the door, "Carl, pack your bags we have to get your out of Kazakhstan now!". "What in the Hell are you mumbling about I spent three million bribing half the population."

"Because of the crimes you are accused of the Ministry considers you "Persona non-grata" apparently the American government made a very strong case and two CIA Agents are arriving at eight this morning to return you to the States". "Give me twenty minutes and I will be ready, I don't care about anything in the suite. By the way where in the heck am I safe from the arm of the law?" "Cambodia, I have your ticket you leave in two hours, here is your new identity, drivers license, and Passport you have passage on a private jet that carries twenty passengers and bypasses customs. The plane leaves at ten this morning."

"Jones, lets go we have a meet at noon they will sign a Warrant that allows us to remove Carl legally, the rented car is waiting down stairs." They picked up the paper work and followed a Police car to the Hotel, "His suite is on the fifth floor just follow us, we don't want any trouble." The Police knocked on the door, "Open up this is the Police we have a warrant for your arrest." There was silence, just as they were about to kick the door in, it opened, "Can I help you?". "Who are you?". "I'm the maid I'm cleaning the rooms". "Where is the tenant?". "I have no idea the front desk said I was to clean the suite. That's all I know". "Son of a Bitch, we have been played."

The two Police men just held their hands up in frustration, "SORRY BOSS, don't know what to tell you we were only doing as we were told." Meanwhile Carl was halfway to Phnom Penh, Cambodia.

At the Ministry, "We had to act as if we would turn Carl over to the Americans or they would have raised hell they accused him of murder and many other crimes, so we played their game and warned him so he could leave the country a few hours ahead of the CIA." Morrison was pissed, "The Government played us I would bet ten to one Carl was forewarned we were coming and he left the country with false ID, probably on a private jet so we can't track him." Jones, "Do you really think the Government is involved in this?" "Hell yes, the word is Carl spread at least three million dollars to get here in the first place, they aren't going to give up the Golden Goose". "Now what?". "I say we call the boss and visit our Embassy in Astana maybe our CIA contact can point us in the right direction." They rented a car and drove to the American Embassy, Morrison had called DC and the Embassy was waiting for them, the CIA Agent met them as they drove in. "Just missed your fish, these people are pretty tricky I have been checking on private jet schedules since your call, if he did take a private jet he is probably in Cambodia by now, also Vietnam, or Myanmar he can get very, very lost in that part of the world". "How about checking for a transfer of funds from one of his offshore accounts". "I can do that, let's go up to my office and I'll see what I can find." They all settled in Charley's office, he opened the liquor cabinet and pulled out a bottle of Premium BURBON, set three glasses on his desk and poured everyone three fingers. "Drink up gentlemen, tomorrow will be a better day." Charley pulled up the schedule for private flights, "Here's one that left around ten this morning for Phnom Penh, Cambodia I have a contact at the airport I'll give him a call maybe he can ID Carl the flight is landing as we speak." "Hey Choy I need you to ID a passenger on the flight from Astana it should be landing anytime now it's a private jet, I've sent his picture to your phone, do not approach under any circumstances he is extremely dangerous, do you copy?". "I hear you boss, will call back if I spot him". "OK, now we just wait I say we go have a bite to eat what do you say?". "Sounds good to us we haven't eaten all day." Morrison hears a beep someone just sent him a text, "What now It's my ex-wife how in the hell did she get this phone number?" Dear Morrison, "it's your daughter's birthday how about sending her some flowers and maybe if you can leave your damned job for a few minutes give her a call, you're such an Ass at times. Your ex-wife, she still loves her Daddy." He smiles and shows Jones the Text, "Always busting my balls!" "From the sound of it you deserve it", and laughed. While they were eating Charley's phone dinged and a picture of Carl appeared on his phone. "Well now you know where he his but your going to have a heck of a time trying to get him out of Cambodia. Oh, by the way my office just called they saw a transfer of ten million dollars from one of his off shore accounts. It was deposited in a bank in Cambodia."

CHAPTER: THIRTY NINE

"We can put a crimp in his style I say we confiscate the ten million, the bank in Cambodia has been identified. We can file a complaint with the Bank but the transfer occurred a couple of hours ago if I were Carl the money would have been withdrawn immediately."

Morrison alerted the CIA to see if there was anyway to reverse the wire transfer. The CIA had their man in Cambodia contact the Bank and find out what could be done to hold the account. To his dismay the money had been transferred to another Bank in Thailand and cashed out, the owner had turned his paper into gold and Bearer Bonds and disappeared. The Embassy in Thailand sent an Agent to the Bank in Thailand and showed the Teller who had cleared the transaction a picture of Carl. "No Sir, the gentlemen who cleared the account appeared to be Oriental I would say Chinese, he had all the necessary paperwork everything was on the up and up." "Have you any idea where the money was transferred?". "No idea! once it is out of our hands the Bank has no more liability". "Morrison we just received a memo from the Thai Embassy". "And what information did it reveal, anything of interest?". "Afraid not the ten million has evaporated and Carl is no where to be found."

Carl settled into his home in Siem Reap, "This will do for now the CIA is probably trying to find my ten million dollars I have friends in China. The American Government has no leverage with the CCP those morons have no idea in the States what goes on, their asleep at the wheel, half the politicians are being paid off to look the other way." He thought back to when he still lived at home, the last person who screwed with me was my father and he didn't live to tell the tale he was a roaring drunk who would beat the shit out of anyone who happened to be in his line of sight when he returned from a bout of drinking. Carl had just turned sixteen and was a strapping six foot, one hundred ninety five pounds. He remembered the night like it was yesterday his father started to beat his mother, then turned on him. Carl allowed his father to strike him twice feeling the rage from years of beatings, he lashed out striking his father and knocking him senseless.

"Mother you have to come with me when he wakes up he will be crazy". "No, I won't leave him!" Carl, "I am packing and I won't be back". "John you want to come with me I'll make sure you are taken care of?" his brother shook his head yes. "Go pack we are out of here, Mom if I hear he has hurt you I will come back and kill him". "Roary, please leave I can handle your father". "Come on John we are leaving."

Carl, watched out for his mother and sister from a distance and one night the bastard beat his mother so badly she almost died. He found him at the nearest club and when he exited he beat him to death with a baseball bat, the satisfaction he felt was amazing, the power to kill. I was not quite seventeen so they put me in a Juvenile Home till I was nineteen, because of my mother they allowed her to take responsibility for me.

When I was twenty I killed a local bum and switched my identification with the bum made sure my drivers license was just scorched and burned the body in an abandoned car. Took his name and moved to LA, went to work for a local drug Lord and became an enforcer for the Drug Cartel I really enjoyed the work and here you are Carl hiding in Cambodia with the CIA up your ass. Carl called his counterpart in Thailand, "Sergi how in the hell are you". "Who is this?". "Carl, you knew I was In Cambodia and expected a call". "Yea,Yea, Carl you are too hot to do business with, it is all over that your Mansion is a graveyard, Carl, Carl you are too hot to handle". "Don't give me that bull I have a need for a couple million dollars worth of Fentanyl mixed with cocaine",there was silence on the other end of the line. "OK, not on the phone, same place as before, click."

He parked a couple clicks from the boarder between Cambodia and Thailand, pulled his Glock and made sure it was loaded.

At one in the morning he saw headlights in the dark, "Probably Sergi." He left his car and took cover behind a stand of trees. The car slowed and the driver shined a spotlight on the parked vehicle, Sergi hollered from the car, "Relax Carl I have the stuff for you, this isn't a setup. The word from the Tong is this will be your territory."

Carl walked slowly from cover but stayed in the shadows, "Sergi you Vodka drinking Ruskie how are you? Now why don't you get slowly out of the car and walk to me and drop the package on the road."

"No problem, brother why so nervous, I'm making the drop alone." "The CIA and God knows who else is after me, I can't be too careful. The entire operation in the States is unraveling. From what I can tell they have been able to spot two of our double agents and they want me for murder and treason". "You can always ask the CCP for asylum". "Not in my genes, don't particularly like Chinese food."

CHAPTER: FORTY

Morrison's encrypted phone beeped, "Hello,Director what can I do for you?"

"I need you and Jones back in LA our interpreters have broken the code of the documents that were uncovered at the Mansion."

There was an Armored SUV waiting at the curb, "The plane leaves at eleven, I say we take a day off and relax, then start putting everything we've found together in the morning."

"Jones, meet me at the Morgue ten this morning I just talked to Adam the Coroner they have been able to identify every victim except two and he thinks he will ID them in a couple of days."

On every table in the Morgue there was a body bag, the temperature was set at sixty degrees, Jones, "Why in the hell is it so damned cold in here and what is that frigging smell?"

Morrison started to laugh, "Number one the temperature keeps the odor of the corpses down and Number two slows the decomposition."

Adam, "Hey Morrison, glad you are here I have ID' the two males, we know one of them was undercover, but the other victim was Oriental and the second in command of a local Tong. He had been tortured whoever worked him over broke all his fingers and busted up his feet, were able to identify him through his Dental records."

"What about the women how did they die, drug overdoses, murdered, heart attacks?"

Adam chuckled, "Three of them were drug overdoses, they had just about every drug known to man in their systems, we checked their hair for extended use two showed they were long term users, one appeared to have been forcibly overdosed."

"What about this Devil Club, did any of the corpses appear to have been ritually murdered?" "Yes, and the strange thing is one of women was a missing employee of a Foreign Embassy in LA. She was definitely murdered."

Jones "What Embassy?", "That's what seems strange the Bulgarian Embassy what in the hell was she doing at the Mansion?". "All I know the Embassy has an APB out looking for her she disappeared six months ago". "Do we know what her job was?". "They were kind of vague, which leads me to believe she was in Intelligence. Maybe she uncovered something that got her killed."

Morrison, thinks I need to check this out something doesn't smell right, he calls the CIA office, "This is Agent Blake who is this and how did you get this number?". "This is Morrison in LA I need to ask you some questions". "Who in the hell are you I'll have your ass arrested". "Relax Agent Blake just call the Director in DC and give him the code name "Red Herring" and he will confirm who I am and what my assignment is". "All I can say is I sure as hell hope Morrison or who ever you are that your on an encrypted phone, because "Red Herring" is Top Secret." "Please just make the call and call me right back, OK."

Ten minutes and Morrisons phone rang, "I don't know who you are but I am to give you any information you ask for, so ask." "Did you plant a Mole in the Bulgarian Embassy? her name was Emilia Ivankovy". "Where in the hell did you get that information?". "Look Blake just answer my question she was found murdered, were you her handler?, because it looks like you did a shit job she was found buried in a concrete slab, along with a dozen other people."

Silence, "OK, what do you want to know?". "Everything I need to know everything". "I turned her and she was feeding me info on how the Embassy was working with the CCP, we had picked up some information from one of the satellites that tied them into the CCP so I turned her". "Well Blake some how her cover was blown and they put her under a foot of concrete". "I just thought she didn't want to play the game anymore". "So you gave her up, you are one big asshole". "I didn't say that". "Didn't have to how else would they know?". "Enough of this what connection did the Embassy have to the Chinese, was the Tong involved?". "Yes, they were bringing in Fentanyl by the pound in their diplomatic pouches and the last I heard before she disappeared, someone in the Embassy was negotiating not with the CCP but with the Tong to bring in weapons". "What type of weapons?". "The ones that can be made out of special materials with a 3D computer, they planned to flood the USA with them." "Did this have anything to do with the Mansion that burned down a while ago, there must be a link because her body was found there and the main suspect has fled to Cambodia."

"We need to put a twenty four hour surveillance on the Embassy,I am sure that they are using a private company to get the contraband out and put it in the hands of a drug dealer and an arms dealer or maybe they are one and the same."

They set up a twenty four hour watch and every Thursday night at eleven in the evening a Van with Contractor lettering would park in the shadows and two men would bring out a number of boxes and load them in the Van."I followed the Van to a warehouse in the south of LA where the boxes were unloaded." "Did you get this on film?"."Yes Sir, and the names of the Embassy employees, we have a couple of undercover men trying to set up a buy as we speak."

CHAPTER: FORTY ONE

Morrison, "We need to have the FBI release Marjorie Swift she was a Black Op and has knowledge of how this Operation works. I will bet she knows a lot more than she is letting on, she is playing it close to the vest, smart girl figured I would need her expertise sooner than later."

Morrison calls the local Bureau of the FBI, "Can I speak to the Senior Special Agent in Charge". "He is on the phone right now can I have him call you back?". "Please leave him this message, I am working on a case with the CIA that is Top Priority and I would appreciate it if he could let me have the use of Marjorie Swift as she a has Black Ops background. Have him call me on my encrypted phone, thank you" he hangs up.

"Boss you just had a call from somebody named Morrison, he wants you to release a Marjorie Swift into his custody, claims it is Top Priority I have his phone number if you want it."

"Haven't a clue what he is talking about don't have time for some CIA Agent looking for who knows what. just leave it on my desk."

Jones, "Have you had a response from the Local FBI yet?" "Not yet, I'll give them another call we need Marjorie I am sure she will be a big help." Phone rings "LA FBI Headquarters."

"This is Agent Morrison I called awhile ago and I am still waiting for an answer I requested that Marjorie Swift be allowed to join my team, can I speak to the Senior Special Agent tell him this concerns an on going investigation code name "Red Herring", so it would be appreciated if he could get back to me, I don't want to have to call DC."

"Boss Agent Morrison called again he said to tell you that he is heading an Investigation code word "Red Herring", and he mentioned calling DC if he doesn't get an answer."

"Give me his number I have not a clue what he is calling about."

"Morrison you have a call from the Local FBI Office." "About time you answered my call Special Agent, when can I have Marjorie Swift?"

"Say what! I just called you as one Bureau to another as a courtesy."

Morrison was getting steamed, apparently the LA Bureau had not been read in, "Special Agent Griffin may we meet face to face, say for lunch and I would like to lay out my case and my need for the release of Marjorie Swift. I have sent you my CIA code you can confirm prior to our meeting."

"Wednesday at twelve the French Restaurant downtown." "Very good Griffin I will be there to state my case."

As he was walking towards the French Restaurant he spotted two Agents at a table along the pedestrian walkway, a female Agent waiting tables and although he couldn't spot him or her a sniper probably across the street on the roof.

Morrison walked to the table with Special Agent Griffin and shook hands.

"Sit down Morrison I have heard nothing but good things about you, interesting you went from a Police Lieutenant to a CIA Agent in charge of your own case the "Red Herring", at the behest of the President of the United States. Yes, I will release Marjorie into your care."

"Look Griffin I don't mean to keep you out but I have specific orders as to who I can coordinate with, if I can get the permission to Read you in I will do it gladly, this is an international problem. I know the FBI has two thousand active cases concerning the CCP at present so maybe the people on top feel you have your hands full."

"She will be at my office in the morning, would recommend an Armored SUV she still has a million dollar bounty on her head."

After lunch Morrison," Thank's for your cooperation, it is appreciated. Will do the Read In when you are approved."

"Lets go Jones, we pick up Marjorie this morning the Armored SUV is waiting for us in the garage, I figured we should be careful in case there is someone trying to collect her bounty."

When they arrived at the FBI Headquarters Marjorie was waiting for them, Morrison signed the paperwork allowing them to take Marjorie. She turned to her FBI handlers,"How about taking off the leg monitor, somebody would be able to follow my every move, you people just don't think, if you were on my team I would have your ass. I thought they sent you people to school?"

"Marjorie, cool it they are doing you and me a favor. At least you will have a few months of freedom while we work on this case."

"OK, OK, I hear you what do you need from me, I thought I was on everyones shit list."

"We have found quite a few bodies buried under the basement slab and on the grounds, plus a safe with papers that seem to connect a number of foreign countries with the Cartel in LA. I need you to do a critique on the victims, we think they are somehow connected to a number of elected officials and wealthy business people."

They all entered the SUV Marjorie in the front passenger seat Morrison drove, Jones occupied the back seat with an armed guard. They drove through town and pulled on the freeway.

Morrison was in the passing lane doing eighty, "We should be on site in thirty minutes, Marjorie I need you to peruse the site, we have placed markers at each of the bodies locations, names, and cause of death."

Marjorie is not answering just sitting there staring ahead. "What's the problem, why so quiet?". "I think we are being followed, I have been watching that pickup truck in the side mirror ever since we left the FBI building. He definitely has been tracking us."

She reaches across the seat and pulls Morrison's Glock from his holster. "I hope this baby is loaded". "Careful Marjorie lets keep cool, I don't need any bad publicity. If they keep their distance don't act we only have a couple of minutes to make the site. As he spoke he noticed the pickup was picking up speed and was closing the gap between them.

"Hey Marjorie our tail is picking up speed, the only way they can take us out is with an RPG and for sure a Nuclear Tipped RPG". "I think they are going to try to cut us off, bet they are hoping we exit at the next turnoff, that's where they plan to ambush us, speed up and pull in front of the truck when he gets close slam on the brakes". "Got you, reach under the seat there's a clip loaded with armor piercing ammo". "Got it!."

Morrison watched the truck it was speeding up trying to cut the SUV off, just as they were almost close enough to cut them off,

Marjorie, "HOLLERED NOW.", Morrison pulled in front of the truck and jammed on the brakes. The brakes from the SUV were burning and smoking, the truck couldn't stop and smashed into the rear of the SUV. "What's happening?" The truck appears to be locked on our rear bumper, Morrison turns hard to the left and then right the hard right tears the bumper off of the truck, causing it to careen, the driver loses control and the truck rolls over at eighty miles an hour crashing into a concrete barrier throwing the passenger onto the highway the driver is trapped in the cab. "Here we go, I'm stopping." He slams on the brakes, "GO, GO," grab the guy laying on the blacktop and I will see to the driver. "Jones and the Guard, jump out of the car and turn the passenger over," "Is he breathing?". "Just barely, careful these crazies will do anything to complete the mission". "Cuff the bastard and drag him out of the road". "What's with the driver? he seems to be conscious." They could smell gas leaking onto the road, "We need to get him out now or he will be toast." An Emergency vehicle and a Fire Engine pulled alongside of the wreckage, "Hey! over here you need to cut the top out of this truck the driver is trapped."

The Emergency crew removed the top and pulled out the driver. Marjorie whispered into Morrison's ear, "These two are in our data base the passenger has a outstanding Warrant for murder and the other one is on our Watch List." The Fire Department covered the truck in foam, Jones opened the rear of the truck, "Holy Shit, look at this." There was a half a dozen RPG's and at least a dozen 3D Machine Guns. "Have the Police block this lane and call in our Team, we need to know if those RPG's are armed with Nuclear Warheads."

CHAPTER: FORTY TWO

*J*ones waited with the bodyguard until the Nuclear Team arrived, "So what do we have?". "Not sure but we figured it would be smart to call your team to see if there is any radioactive materials in the truck before it was removed. With all the crazy business going on lately."

He pointed his Geiger Counter at the rear of the truck and it went crazy, "Every one don gear we have a very radioactive situation, hey Jones and your buddy back away. Mack check these two they may be contaminated."

One of the Hazmat Team checked them for contamination, "the count was fairly high, You need to strip now and get in the shower, leave your clothes in the bags in the Trailer soap and rinse at least twice. My people will supply you with clean clothes."

Jones called Morrison, "Hey we are contaminated you will have to be checked before you enter the Mansion site, we just stripped and washed be careful". "Are you shitting me, Marjorie call in a Hazmat Team to check us for Radiation."

Morrison pulled over just outside of the perimeter of the Mansion and waited for the team.

They had some reading but nothing like Jones, "You need to get rid of your clothes and wash down, we'll have to take the SUV and wash it out with a special chemical, I will send you a clean SUV and new clothes" they stripped down and washed in the portable showers in the trailer and donned clean overalls. "Marjorie lets walk to the site it will be a couple of hours before they bring us a SUV and a clean set of duds."

Morrison questioned the Agent in Charge, "Any thing new Charley?" "Not a thing Boss, we gridded the property and went over every inch three times. Twenty bodies is it and the safe, this place gives me the creeps."

"I know what you mean. I want you to leave two men here twenty four hours a day change shifts every four hours and move our snipers on the ridge every two hours I have a feeling we will see these people again, just a hunch I have a gut feeling we are missing something."

Marjorie, "What the hell is going? on it's almost as if we are being invaded."

"We are, the last Administration looked the other way and let our enemies run rampant. Now we are playing catchup."

"I could really sink my teeth into this I owe you Morrison big time, thank you. Hopefully I will be exonerated in the near future and kick ASS!"

The New SUV arrived and they headed back into LA and the Morgue. "I want you to see if you can identify any of our victims, we have profiled some of them, but if you have had personal contact it would be great."

Marjorie walked into the Morgue and shook hands with Adam the Coroner, she looked around commenting, "JESUS, This looks like a frigging massacre. How many bodies in all?" "Twenty mostly women, we have a total of sixteen women and four men, we still haven't been able to identify three of the women and two of the men."

She just shook her head thinking, "That son of a bitch Carl was planning to make me number twenty one, I should have killed him when I had the chance, my greatest wish is that I will meet him again and complete the job."

"OK, Adam lets start, I will let you know if I need time to recognize anyone."

Marjorie took her time, "The first three were prostitutes and four of the women worked in the restaurant they probably were lured in and killed. There is more to this than they think I have seen some of these women as escorts for Politicians and a few Millionaires in the city."

"So what do you think Marjorie? Is there a conspiracy to kill women or am I crazy."

"There is no doubt there is something that is not right, what is wrong with people this isn't the Dark Ages this is the Twenty First Century, how in the hell can civilized human beings sacrifice each other?"

"You got me Marjorie, let's get back to the job. You have any feel about the four men we found in the slab", "well we know that one of them was part of a drug ring, one was an undercover agent working for the ATF he was probably outed and killed, the other two I have not a clue."

Morrison, "We are still working on identifying who they are the Pathologist is checking dental records hopefully we will know in a day or two."

"Can I ask you a question?"

"Anything, just ask if I can help I will." "Can you put pressure on the FBI to wrap up the case against me I am innocent, there is a mole in the organization and until he or she is uncovered a lot more people will die."

"I'll see what I can do I believe you Marjorie, you were set up, when this is over I will give you a glowing report and I will personally follow up on your case. Come on I'll take you to the Motel, get a good nights sleep." The next morning Morrison picked up Marjorie, "Morning I have good news they have identified both men from dental records". "So what's their background, one of them was a Federal Agent looking to charge Carl and his Company with tax evasion, the other was just a small contractor that did renovations. We are backtracking and setting up a timeline as to where the Agent was last seen. My guess is he found out what Carl was into and had him snuffed out."

"I say we are looking for someone or maybe two people that worked for Carl and did his dirty work." Morrison just looked at her, "When I was working for the scum bag there was two guys who Carl always called to do his dirty work, they were from the South side and I remember him on the phone cursing out some nosey Federal Agent trying to get a Warrant for his company records and he wanted the stupid bastard taken care of."

"Do you have any idea where those two hang out?" "The last I heard they hung out at a place called the the "Bloody Bucket" it's a pretty rough joint, but the food is good". "When's the last time you saw them?". "Just before Carl tried to bury me in the concrete". "Do you have any idea where this place is?,I say we go for a ride and scope the place out."

Morrison calls Jones, "Hey bud send me one of the Rangers guarding the site, make sure he is big and dressed in civvies." "Gotcha, he will meet you at the site in an hour."

"You Morrison?". "And you are Master Sergeant Smith". "Yes, Sir they said you wanted a body guard, I can kill a man six ways before they know they are dead". "Very good Sergeant, but hopefully we won't have to kill, I want to take them alive so I can question them". "Let's go, I love a good fight". "Sergeant relax, please just relax."

"Marjorie you drive, Aren't you afraid I'll try to escape?" "No, You want back in I have complete faith in you, I have a feeling when you are exonerated they will kick you upstairs, I need you on my team." The trip took forty five minutes, "The Bloody Bucket is just around the corner." She pulled into the parking lot and parked. "We're looking for an Ape called Nick and Two Fingers they both are over six foot tall and probably around two fifty to three hundred pounds, very nasty, nasty boys." When they entered the Bloody Bucket there was standing room only at the bar, "Jesus, You can't see through the smoke and the place smells like stale beer." Marjorie, "There they are sitting at the far table playing cards. The two Apes in suits, be careful they are probably packing and I have no idea who the other three are playing cards with them". "Sergeant are you armed?". "Yes sir, and wearing a vest". "Very good take the left Marjorie and I will go right." Nick looked up, "Two Fingers, guess who is here and she brought two friends?" he reached into his coat and started to pull his weapon. Smith had them covered in seconds, "Please don't gentlemen, just slowly put your hands on the table and you three stand up slowly and back out of the bar, all we want to do is talk." Nick looked around and standing there was Marjorie and Morrison with guns pointed at them. "Marjorie how in the hell are you?, I missed you we should get together sometime."

CHAPTER: FORTY THREE

"Hey, Nick kiss my ass, the only place we'll get together is when I put you two assholes behind bars, these two gentlemen have questions to ask and if you want to stay out of jail don't bullshit us." Morrison, "We should go to my office, I would prefer not to cuff you two. Please stand up, and Marjorie check them for weapons". "Gladly" she dropped four Glocks on the table and a six inch knife. "OK, Let's walk slowly out of the bar" He looked around the bartender had his hands concealed and the three poker players were blocking the door.

Sergeant Smith had his back to the wall and pointed his weapon at the bar tender, "Hey Jack, slowly put your hands on the bar or I will put a bullet between your eyes, and you three move away from the door." Just when it seemed that they were going to have a shootout, there was the sound of a weapon being cocked. "Everyone stay where they are and don't move." Morrison looked over his shoulder and there stood an entire Swat Team. "Damn Morrison, you should know better than try to bring in these two without backup, I would bet everyone in this dung hole has an outstanding warrant pending." Everyone in the bar backed against the wall raising their hands. "Good, now don't try anything and you won't get hurt, you two, There's a SUV outside my men will take you to the Compound for questioning, this is a Federal matter, so I recommend that everyone disappear before the Federal Marshalls show up." The two prisoners were placed in the SUV and shackled, when they arrived at the Compound were placed in an Interrogation Room and cuffed to a steel bar welded to the table. "You Boys, get settled we'll be in to question you, we need to know what you did for the Cartel, who gave you orders and who was involved?, laid a pad and pencil on the table, write the information down. I'll be back in a couple of minutes."

The Team stood watching the screen, "Give them a few minutes they will start talking."

"Nick what have you got us into? you said no-one would ever know."

"Just don't get your shorts screwed up, they don't know nothing, so keep your mouth shut."

"Those bastards are going to sell us down the river unless we drop the dime on the Cartel."

"I said, "SHUT UP" you asshole they are probably listening to everything we say."

Morrison, "Ok Jones, now we separate them and send in Marjorie to interrogate Two Fingers". "You sure?". "Yes! do it." The door to the Interrogation Room opens two Rangers enter. "Two Fingers you come with us and Nick stays."

Two Fingers stands up and leaves the room and the two Rangers follow. The door slams, Nick jumps as the door slams. Two Fingers has been sitting in the Interrogation Room for forty five minutes handcuffed to the table, "Hey, hey I have to piss how about giving me a break. I'll tell you anything you want to know." The door opens, Marjorie walks in and sits down across from him. "The Guards will be in and take you to the john, then when you come back we can have a long talk." after the trip to the john he is escorted in sits down raises his hand to be cuffed to the bar. "That's OK, he doesn't have to be cuffed", Marjorie waves the guard off, "You can leave us alone". "But Ma'am he's a known killer". "Please, do as I ask, I'll be alright." The Guard shakes his head and leaves the room, stands outside with another Guard just in case, Two Fingers would try something. "Two Fingers, how are you? You look well where in the hell did Carl disappear to? and don't give me a load of horse shit. You be square with me and I will have them put you in a Relocation Program". "Hell Marjorie, they will kill me as soon as I walk into a jail cell tonight." Marjorie just sits staring at Two Fingers, he is sitting shaking, there is sweat running down his forehead. She thinks, "He is scared shitless, I have to get him talking, but how? I have to convince him we can keep him alive". "Look, I can have you under guard twenty four hours and after we get your deposition you will disappear, but I need you to tell me everything because if they find you left something out or lied you will be fed to the dogs, do you understand?". "I started to work a couple of years ago for Carl he was into sex and drugs. I was hired as a fixer when someone started something I fixed it one way or another. Then last year he met with some Chinese and all of a sudden we were dealing in weapons and when the last shipment arrived there were Nuclear Tipped RPG's and the North Koreans supplying women, I wanted to get the hell away from Carl, I knew Nick could care less what we did. Two of our guys disappeared and were found floating in the river they were skimming and Carl personally put a bullet in them and dumped them in the drink. The Lawyer was into it up to his neck he went to China and thats when all hell broke loose. The Cabal was bringing in Fentanyl by the pound, White Slavery, weapons that would be used for war, you name it, this Government does not have a clue, they are planning Sedition and they plan to take over the Government." Marjorie calls Morrison and Jones, "I am going to need you to find a new home for our friend Two Fingers, he may look stupid but I tell you he has a keen eye for detail." "So who Did he give up?". "Everybody, I am having his statement transcribed as we speak". "Sounds like you hit the jackpot, Marjorie."

CHAPTER: FORTY FOUR

Two Fingers was removed and placed in Solitary Confinement temporally till they could set him up for Relocation. "It's Nicks turn in the barrel, I say you take him Jones, let's see how he cries and moans about being abused by the Government". "Yea, according to the guards he has been threatening to sue since we locked him up, he claims we don't have any evidence against him. Everything is Two Fingers fault and he can prove it, just ask him". "Bring him to the Interrogation Room and cuff him, turn on the Air Conditioning and let him set for awhile maybe that will cool him off." They watched on the monitor as Nick was cuffed to the steel bar, he immediately started to complain, "It's cold in here, turn up the heat this is torture, I'll complain to the United Nations." Jones walked into the Interrogation Room smiling, placed a recorder on the table and sat facing the prisoner. "Nick please state your name, date of birth, and present address." Jones laid a half a dozen pictures on the table, "Do you recognize any of these people". "Don't recognize anyone". "You don't know anyone in any of these pictures?" Jones then placed two pictures on the table and there was Nick with his arms around the two women and shaking hands with one of the men". "I, I may have met them once or twice, but I can't remember their names."

"Didn't you meet with them to close a drug deal six months ago and they all were found dead, and Carl paid you an extra one hundred thousand dollars as a bonus for setting them up so he could get rid of the local competition? we found their bodies in an oil tank buried at a deserted factory building."

The blood drained out of Nick's face, "Look I didn't know he was going to kill them". "You really expect me to believe that, we pinged your cell phone and it shows you were within half a mile from the site, when they disappeared. Two Fingers,"Said Carl and you were supposed to meet the victims that night and they all disappeared."

"Two Fingers is the killer I never had anything to do with murders, he's trying to frame me". "Really, he has an air tight alibi and his phone shows he was twenty miles away at a Night Club, we even have film with a time stamp showing he wasn't any where near the crime scene". "Your ass is grass, we have you as an accessory to at least four murders, you better start talking. Right now the death penalty is on the table. If you want to cut a deal I want to know everything that Carl and the Cartel was into especially how the Tong and Russian Mafia are involved." He slid a pad and pencil across the table, "I'll get us coffee and give you a few minutes to think about it." Jones walked out of the room and joined the others to watch Nick over the monitor, Morrison and Marjorie were standing there watching. Marjorie screamed, "Get a guard in there the bastard is going to commit suicide". "What in the hell are you talking about he's, Ok", just as Jones spoke Nick took the pencil and jammed it in his jugular vein and started to grind the point into his flesh. She took off running, knocking Jones down on his knees and crashed through the Interrogation Room door, grabbing Nicks arm throwing him to the floor. Morrison and Jones were frozen like deer in the headlights. "Don't just stand there get a frigging medic in here now before he bleeds to death" she put pressure on the wound afraid to remove the pencil that he would surely bleed out. The Medics entered the room, "Move out, and let us take over they immediately gave Nick a shot to put him to sleep and stopped the bleeding. Marjorie, "Get him to the hospital and put a twenty four hour guard on him, I want him shackled to the bed. I'll be there to check within the hour". "Yes, sir will do." Morrison walked into the room after they removed Nick, "How in the hell did you know he was going to try to commit suicide?" "I had a prisoner who was the head of intelligence for a group of Terrorists and he pulled the same game on me, the only problem was he succeeded. When I saw Nick pick up the pencil the point was not so he could start writing but was pointed at his neck, I knew he planned to take his own life, we need to keep him alive he is a valuable asset." Simons phone dinged, he opened the message "Nick on way to Hospital in Ambulance, stop at all cost". "Mickey get the RPG we have to move, they were waiting a city block from the Safe House the Ambulance would have to drive in their direction as the street was one way. He carefully positioned the Van so he would have a clean shot at the Ambulance, slid the side panel open and waited, the Ambulance was traveling about fifty miles an hour he placed the RPG into position and as it passed fired directly into the side of the vehicle. There was a flash and a sonic boom, the Ambulance was thrown straight up in the air and danced a Death Dance careening like a Childs toy as it smashed into the pavement rolling over and over landing against a stone barrier and exploded. The van was too close to the target and the implosion caved in the side of the van killing the shooter and set off the C4 in the rear of the vehicle, killing the three attackers and incinerating their bodies. The last thing the shooter thought was, "The boss was right I did have the Van too close to the target", as he was engulfed in the inferno.

CHAPTER: FORTY FIVE

The explosion rocked the Headquarters, "What in the hell was that?" They all ran to the windows to see the Ambulance flying through the air.

"How in the hell did they know who was in the Ambulance? we have a Deep Mole in our Organization, we need to clean this up now." Morrison, "Keep cool, Jones check to see if anyone made a cell phone call in the last few minutes, maybe we can pin down who the Traitor is."

Marjorie was pissed, "I've been telling you from day one we have a frigging Mole in the Organization and nobody believed me and now this. How did they know?, we have been set up, somehow they were made aware that we had these two in custody and were laying in wait, hell we could have all been killed, they set up a Box type Ambush, Morrison we are being played big time."

Jones, "Can't find anything, it doesn't appear anyone in the building sent a message to the attackers."

There was the scream of Emergency sirens and Police cars. Morrison called Sergeant Smith, "We need a couple dozen men to cordon off the area, you keep watch on everyone block off the scene.

Take pictures, names and identify everyone at the crash site. I don't care if they are a General or Congress Man or Women make them show proof."

"Yes Sir, will do" He calls to his men, "Lets go boys we have a job to do, everybody in battle gear, take extra ammo, we need to secure the site and identify the enemy, move it, move it!!"

Within minutes the entire Company was on the move, Sergeant Smith placed snipers on the roof tops, met with the Lieutenant of the Local Police and explained the circumstances.

"Sorry Lieutenant I need your identification and he took his picture,"Is all this necessary?"

"Absolutely, this is Top Secret everyone here will have to swear to secrecy. No, reporters if this is leaked heads will roll."

Morrison looked around for Marjorie, "Jones where is Marjorie?". "I think she left with Sergeant Smith, last I saw he was saluting her calling her Captain Swift apparently they know each other." Marjorie had suited up, wearing a bullet proof vest and signed out a M249 Light Machine Gun from the Armory.

"What is your take on this mess" Sergeant, "I say we were compromised there is definitely someone in your outfit that is leaking Intelligence, and this is just the beginning of a whole lot of bullshit, I can see it coming."

Marjorie, "I think you should deploy a squad half way up the block and another at your rear I'll leave it up to you how you place them". "Yes Sir Captain will do, glad to have you back." Morrison walks to the site, "Marjorie you are in your glory, I sure as hell hope they clear you in the near future I can see how you are one resource I can't do without."

"Hey boss we picked a message that emanated from inside the Compound, but we couldn't pinpoint it."

He looks at his phone, "All good, enemy destroyed." "Any survivors?"

"None!"

He put the burn phone in his pocket thinking, "Can't ditch it in the compound someone will find it."

"It's coming from the lower office". "what's coming from the lower office?". "Who ever is texting from the compound". "Send Security there now, maybe we can catch the bastard."

The Security Guards kicked the door open, "The place is empty, what the hell, they must have just left, we missed him." Morrison calls Jones,"Hey, Jones did you see anyone in the lower office?". "No, I have been monitoring the top floor, why do you ask?". "Just checking, no problem."

Marjorie,"What was that all about?". "Nothing in particular, why don't you check the security cameras in the lower hallway, just in case."

Marjorie enters the Security Area, "Close the door and lock it." "You hard of hearing? I said close the door and lock it."

"But that is only allowed when we go to Code Red." "What world do you live in? we are at Code Red, we just had a prisoner assassinated and an Ambulance blown to pieces, the Compound is under siege. Like I said lock the frigging door or I will and if I do, your head will be the door stop."

"Yes Sir, door closed and sealed."

She has the Tech run the security film from the top floor to the lower level,"now run it back to an hour ago on the first floor and ahead in slow motion. Stop who is that in the hallway?" "It's hard to tell can't see his face". "Drop the camera lower and check his gait, he is a slow walker and leaning to the left. That's OK, just wanted to check the area to be safe."

"Unlock the Security Door, I'll see myself out, have a nice day." She mumbled to herself, "Should I tell Morrison? I could't see his face he probably wouldn't believe me anyway. I have to be positive. Maybe set a trap so he exposes himself."

She opens the office door and just stands smiling.

"What is on your mind little lady?". "Just thinking, we should smoke our spy out by setting a trap". "Do you have anybody in mind?". "Lets just say I have someone targeted, I think we should check out everyone with a Top Security Clearance and start with me."

"Are you sure?". "Yes, absolutely, I was with you when the first text was detected and with Sergeant Smith when the second one was sent. I saved Nick from committing suicide, some one in the Compound warned the Attackers that Nick was in the Ambulance heading in their direction, I sure as hell wasn't in the lower office when the second text was sent."

CHAPTER: FORTY SIX

Morrison calls Jones, "I need your burn phone we are checking all communication devices, someone in this Compound is alerting the Enemy" Jones, "What you think I have been turned?" "Just place it on the table, please."

Jones reaches into his pocket and lays the phone on the table. "Now your encrypted phone," "What is this shit?". "Just do as I ask we are all under suspicion". "Marjorie is next and then me, after us, we inspect every one and their phones in the building. I have called a building shutdown no one leaves till we find who is leaking information."

"Sergeant Smith I want you to seal this Compound now, no one is to leave till I say so. I don't care who they are, understand." "Yes Sir."

Marjorie picked up Jones phones and checked them for messages. "May I ask what you need with a Burn Phone Agent Jones?", "just a precaution in case my other phone is compromised, it has a fail safe code built in that will cause it to self implode if it falls into the wrong hands."

"What were you doing in the lower floor office an hour ago?" "I wasn't on the lower floor an hour ago, I told you I was checking out the top floors". "There is footage on a Security Camera shows you walking out of the office on the lower floor at the same time the Ambulance was bombed."

"Can't be, I told you where I was, there must be some mistake." "Lets take a walk and check out the Cameras" Jones, "Absolutely!" Every one walked to the Security Room, Marjorie rang the buzzer to gain entrance, she rang again, no response.

"Morrison do you have the code to open the door?". "Yes," he enters the code and does a visual scan, the door still does not open, "What in the hell is going on here?". "I'll call Security we may have had a breech." Morrison, "Yes, we need someone here immediately there appears to be a lapse in security." Two Security Guards arrive and attempt to open the door, no luck. "Is there any other way into the room?". "There is an emergency panel in the other room I'll enter the code, there is something very wrong going on."

Morrison punches in the code a wall panel opens, "Marjorie you will be able to enter through the opening easier than one of us." She crawled through the opening stood up as soon as she had gained access to the room. There lay the Tech on the floor with a bullet in his head, "SON OF A BITCH, that isn't the some person I talked to awhile ago," she hit the building alarm and all the doors and windows automatically closed, she manually opened the door letting Morrison and Jones enter.

"What is going on?". "Take a look the real Tech is laying on the floor with a bullet in his head, that's not who I originally talked to. I pulled the alarm we have a major breech."

Sergeant Smith arrived with two armed Rangers, "What the hell is happening?" Morrison, "Leave one man here, check all the doors and windows there is an assassin on the loose in our compound, he will kill anyone who is in his way, somehow he circumvented our security. I want him alive."

There was a loud explosion that rocked the building, windows shattered, ceiling tiles crashed to the floor, everyone covered their face to keep from breathing in the dust, "What now? This is not going to be a good day." Marjorie took off running. "I'll bet they blew a hole in one of the windows or steel doors and is attempting to escape." She heard automatic machine gun fire on the second level, then it sounded like a Glock, "I wonder who has the machine gun?" Marjorie placed a clip in her machine gun still running towards the sound of gun fire, looking over her shoulder she saw Morrison and Jones right behind her with guns drawn. When the trio arrived at the main corridor a Ranger a was on the floor wounded, she grabbed his arm and pulled him out of the line of fire, she ripped open the wounded Rangers shirt and put a tourniquet on his arm to stop the bleeding, "He mumbled there are two of them a man and woman, both armed. They tried to take down a door no luck, now have C4 against an exterior bullet proof window". "Where are the other troops, blockaded on the other end of the hall and are cutting through the door as we speak." Marjorie snuck a mirror around the corner, she could see a woman placing the C4 against the reinforced glass. She turned to Morrison "I recognize her she is the receptionist, she is Chinese and the man with her is the other Tech I questioned in the Room concerning the security cameras." Morrison called Sergeant Smith, "How many men do we have outside?". "Two Squads." "Have them move to the front of the building, but be aware they are trying to blow the window with C4 tell them to keep out of range, the blast could blow the terrorists up if they are not careful." Marjorie, "If that C4 is detonated in that confined space we will be peeling both of them off of the wall." Marjorie looked around the corner the man opened fired in her direction taking out the partition. She crawled to the corner and used her mirror to get a bead on the shooter, took a deep breath and fired, the man had a surprised look on his face as he grabbed his chest coughing up blood and fell face first to the floor dead. "GOT YOU, YOU SON OF A BITCH."

The woman had the C4 attached to the window and inserted the cap. Marjorie, "Hey there, why don't we talk you can't get away and if you set off the C4 we will have to vacuum your corpse off the wall that would be very messy". "You Americans need to die I fight for my country". "Well the only one dying today is you, your partner is dead, we can make some kind of deal, what do you say?" she looked at Marjorie not answering. Morrison, "Sergeant Smith what is your position?". "We have breached the door and are ready to move". "Jesus, stay where you are she has armed the C4 the explosion could take you and you'r men out if the backdraft catches you in the hall. I'll let you know when to move. I'm trying to talk her down."

CHAPTER: FORTY SEVEN

"Susie think about it, you aren't getting away. If you set off that C4 in the hall it will kill you. Your partner is dead but you'r still alive, we can give you a safe place to live." Susie, "They will put my family in a Concentration Camp and work them to death if they know I had turned on the Party."

"Just place the detonator on the floor and walk this way very slowly, keep your hands on the top of your head, fingers interlocked, the CCP will think you were killed, we'll give you a new identity, new name, a place to live."

Susie slowly placed the detonator on the floor, she was crying. "They told me the American's would never know, and if I did as told my father would be released from hard labor."

"Stop, and kneel facing me, keep your fingers interlocked, don't move."

Marjorie walked slowly toward Susie, and handcuffed her. "Stand up so I can check for weapons, don't try anything or you will regretted it." She called to the Squad in the outer hall, "Sergeant Smith, It's all clear, get that C4 the hell out of here." They disarmed the explosive and removed it from the building. Susie was placed in detention and cuffed to the wall. "OK, who wants to question her?" Morrison, "My turn, you two check her background, how in the Hell did she get a job with the CIA?". "I'll bet she was a sleeper. She was born here or brought in at a young age and brain washed." Morrison walked in to the Detention Cell and just stood staring at Susie hc placed her file on the bed, flipped it open "how much is truth?" he smirked. "Lets start from the beginning, what do you remember about your childhood?". "I was adopted by a Caucasian family I think I was two years old, they Home Schooled me till I was twelve, then I was sent to a Private School that was anti-American, everyone was taught a foreign language, we were taught how to falsify documents, how to make drops, they paid for us to go to College we were groomed all our lives. I was told that if I didn't do as I was told my family would be tortured and sent to a Concentration Camp." Morrison walked out of the cell and called over the guard, "I want a twenty four hour watch on her, she needs to be fully debriefed as soon as possible."

He walked down the hall and opened his phone, "Marjorie where is Sergeant Smith?". "He's defusing the bomb."

"Tell him I want two men to guard Susie I have a gut feeling she is a marked woman. She has to be guarded twenty four hours I want a guard with her when she goes to take a piss. I have a feeling we are on the verge of breaking the case and she is the key."

Marjorie, "Looks at the phone," Sounds like Morrison is on to something really big."

Jones, "I need you to look into Susie's background who her adopted parents were, where she went to school, especially high school, and college. We will meet tomorrow at one and critique all the information we have on how our Susie was allowed to infiltrate the CIA. We may still have a major problem."

Sergeant Smith and two of his Rangers walked into the jail. "Where is the guard?". "She is supposed to have someone watching her. Hey Boys, get your asses to her cell and check to make sure she is ok, any food get it away from her, we will personally supply her meals."

"Sergeant, Sergeant the guard is dead, it looks like someone caved in his head". "Quick get to the cell."

They ran down the steps and just as they reached the jail floor spotted someone opening Susie's cell door. Sergeant, "Stop him, shoot the bastard, don't let him get to her he's going to kill her."

Sergeant Smith pulled his Automatic emptied his weapon, the intruder fell dead halfway into the cell. Susie was screaming and crying all at the same time, "OH GOD, don't let him kill me."

They helped her out of the cell, "How was he able to gain entrance to her cell?" the guard was moaning as he came to Sergeant Smith, "Help the guard up he had a bad wack on the head but who let the intruder in?" Guard, "I need to see a Doctor, go to the Hospital". "I don't think so you are staying in the compound, that's OK, I think we have a Medic on site that can take care of your superficial wound, by the way how did he gain entrance to the area" Guard, "I don't know what you mean". "I just wondered what you were paid to turn Traitor or have you always been a turncoat?". "You are crazy he threatened me with a gun, said he would kill me if I didn't let him in."

"Really, he was going to shoot you through a steel door, now that would have been quite a feat. Throw this moron in a cell and lock the door, take his belt so he don't hang himself." Sergeant Smith calls

Morrison, "Where do you want us to take Susie so she is safe?". "Bring her to my office and put guards at all entrances, she knows too much they want her dead." Morrison calls, Marjorie and Jones and fills them in on what is going on with Susie. They all meet in Morrison's office and there is Susie sitting on his couch crying.

"Another couple of minutes and she would have been dead, my gut told me something wasn't right, when I talked to the guard, so I alerted Sergeant Smith to check on her."

Marjorie, "How did your accomplice get access to the building, just answer or we will throw you to the wolves. I am sure you won't last an hour on the street."

"They will kill my child, if I talk."

"You don't have any children I checked your physical report, you were never pregnant."

"So let's start over again, where are your adoptive parents?"

CHAPTER: FORTY EIGHT

The Team Checked into Susie's background, she had been adopted by a family living in Virginia when she was two years old she was an orphan her family had been killed in an earthquake in Sichuan, China she had no living relatives.

Her adoptive parents were Tom and Martha Smithon her father had passed away ten years ago, but her mother Martha was still alive living in a Nursing Home located just south of DC.

The Team met the next day and conferred on what to do next. Jones, "I think I have a good idea what Private School her parents sent her to, it is still in business we should see if we can put a plant in the school and when we have enough to close them down, move in and confiscate all their paperwork. I also have a list of the teachers at the school from the time Susie was schooled till today."

Marjorie, "The background on her parents is real, real thin I was able to trace them about five years prior to Susie being adopted." It's like they just appeared out of nowhere living in Virginia with no prior history I think they were smuggled into the USA and were Spymasters, from what I can tell they gave large donations to a number of Senators and were invited to quite a few meetings concerning American Security and were paid as consultants to set up protocols to protect our computer and satellite systems. I need to do a lot more searching into their background and will visit Martha Smithon to see if I can get her to talk." Morrison, "I don't believe anything Susie has said to date. Number One, she doesn't have any living relatives, so her weeping about killing any of her relatives is a typical spy looking for sympathy if she talks it will be all lies. Number Two, she has never been pregnant, so she sure as hell doesn't have a baby we checked her blood work and DNA, nadda, her entire story is nothing, bullshit!!, we need to slap her ass in solitary until she gives up her comrades. Did anyone search her for cyanide?" Agent, "We searched her clothes and checked the teeth everything was clean". "Send in a couple of Female Guards strip her, burn the clothes I mean everything shoes, hair, undergarments, enema, I guarantee she is hiding something."

"OK People, you all know what we have to do, Marjorie you check the mother at the Nursing Home and warn Homeland Security about the consequences of using the Smithon's protocols." The Head of Homeland Security, "Boss there's a CIA Special Agent Marjorie Swift on an Encrypted Line, said she has to talk to you it is imperative she speak to you". "Put her on". "What can I do for you CIA Agent Swift?". "It is our under understanding that your people have been using Smithons encryption protocols." "Smart people we just started to incorporate them into our malware." Marjorie, "Director we have Intelligence they have infiltrated the Government, those Protocols will allow our enemies to penetrate the Defense Systems, they are spies." "Are you sure?". "Absolutely we are in the process of shutting down an entire spy ring." Director, "Will scrub our equipment immediately" the Director called his people to remove any information supplied by the Smithons Corporation.

"I will take care of our Miss Susie and see if I can have her expose any more secrets." Morrison, "Jones, visit the school see what you can find out, we can't take the time to insert a plant it will take too much time. I will get a Federal Judge to issue a FISA Warrant to attach everything at the school. We need to act ASAP." Jones called a Federal Judge and explained the circumstances to the Chief of Staff, "You will have a FISA Warrant by morning." Morrison, "Three teams will surround and arrest everyone in the School." Jones met with the Team Leader, "We go in Saturday morning at three am, most of the students will be absent, but my intel is that the Teachers will be there for a conference, after we round them up I'll let you know who we question and who we release, please no casualties". "Yes Sir, no casualties sir." The Advance Team disarmed the Schools alarm systems, electronic sensors around the perimeter of the property and jammed all signals to their cell phones.

"At two forty five," Jones here. "All their systems have been disabled, we are ready to go." Jones gave the signal, "We move now, let's go men." Squad Two guarded all the exits and windows, Squad One entered the rear and front of the building, all transportation was to be booted. Jake, "Lock them on the tires to stop anyone from attempting to escape in their automobiles." The doors were breeched and Team Two took control of the offices, Team One after disabling the autos, entered the Complex where the Head Mistress and Teachers slept. "Alright Boys and Girls, rise and shine you asses are mine." he kicked in the door to the School Head, and rolled her out of bed and placed her in cuffs, "What is going on, who are you people?" "We are from Homeland Security this school is to train Terrorists how to infiltrate our Sovereign Government, you are under arrest". "You can't do this I have friends in high places". "No, problem we'll be looking at them also". "We need you to unlock all your files, so if you be nice enough to follow us we will search your office and confiscate all of your paperwork". "I refuse, I want a lawyer". "I don't think you understand, we have a FISA Warrant you will be held for forty eight hours before we have to let you have access to Legal advice". "If you don't open the files we will just do what is necessary to open them and I will guarantee it will be a real mess." Jones, "We have six SUV's to transport the School staff to the Compound to be fingerprinted and questioned, there are about twenty students that didn't go home this weekend, what do we do with them?". "I say we question them and call their parents to come pick them up, I'll call the Judge to see if we can legally fingerprint the students." Marjorie, "Judge we just served the FISA Warrant the problem is there we have twenty children in tow, can we legally finger print them without their parents present?". "you need the parents consent my recommendation is call their parents. If they refuse to allow you to finger print the children keep them at the school so the parents can pick them up." They backed the box truck up to the door and started loading all the School files. "Hey, boss we are going to need another truck for the files, the computers and cell phones won't fit." The Staff were transported to the Compound and placed in separate areas under guard. The Students parents were called and asked for permission to question their children, those that agreed were asked to return on Monday morning. The parents that resisted, their children were released. "We will check the families that refused, just in case they have questionable backgrounds". "I wonder how Marjorie is making out with Susie's mother?"

CHAPTER: FORTY NINE

Marjorie drove to the Nursing Home and Parked, she went to the desk and asked for Martha Smithon. "She's in room 110 I believe she is having Physical Therapy I will let her know there is someone her to see her, who should I say is visiting?". "Just tell her it's Marjorie Swift I'm a friend of her daughter Susie wanted me to check in on her mother." The phone at the station rang, "Yes, she is a friend of your daughter, you will be in your room in fifteen minutes send her down and have her wait for me". "Did you hear that Miss Swift she will meet you in her room?". "Go down this corridor and turn left, it's the second room on the right." Marjorie had a gut feeling, "This old broad is going to waylay me, there is some code word that will let her know everything is Ok." She stopped at the door and hesitated, then knocked, "Come in my Dear any friend of my daughters is a friend of mine." Marjorie pushed the door open slowly and there sat Martha holding a Glock17 pointed at her head.

"Well, well, Miss Swift is it, what can I do for you? did you think I was a old woman with Alzheimer's, state your case and leave if you attempt to take me into custody I will put a bullet right between your pretty blue eyes." Marjorie, "Really Mrs. Smithon is it, may I ask what is your real name in Russian.

We know you and your husband were planted by the Russian Secret Service years ago and you worked with the MSS, China's Spy Agency to bring in Susie to use her as a plant in our country." "If you know everything what do you want with me?"

"I would like to bring you in and have you tell us how you and your husband communicated with your handlers. We have your adopted daughter in custody and she has given us a lot of Intel we are working on". "You really think after all this time I am going to give up my Handlers, you aren't playing with a full deck. So, leave or try to arrest me. As for my Susie she is well trained, I doubt she would reveal anything, you Americans are fools we are everywhere."

"Martha, why don't you put down the gun, you are making me nervous, especially when your hands shake". "Let me be real clear we have closed the school where the children are trained, we have the names of everyone who has ever attended the school, the teachers are all in custody and being questioned as we speak, all of the students parents are under surveillance or being arrested". "I will say you are through." She placed the Glock in her lap and sighed, "I'm too old to die this way, I thought when I signed myself into the Home I would be free from all the pressures and just spend my last years in peace."

"Well depending what you tell us we will make sure you spend the rest of your days on one of the Islands listening to the sound of waves as the water splashes on your feet." She places the Glock on the bureau, holds her hands out for Marjorie to cuff her, "Alright now we walk out of here very slowly." She called Morrison, "I need an Armored SUV at the Nursing Home I'm bringing in Martha Smithon, she has agreed to cooperate with us."

"The SUV is on the way, keep her inside till we arrive, they may be monitoring us, be careful." The SUV pulled up to the front of the Home, Marjorie looked out the window something didn't look right. No Morrison, and the Car just sat there waiting, she dialed Morrison, "Where are you?". "We are Twenty Minutes out, why?". "There is a SUV sitting at the curb, we have to use the encrypted phones from now on, I'll keep her safe until you arrive." The SUV pulled away from the curb and drove from the property, disappearing down the tree lined road.

Morrison arrived at the Home as the unknown Auto disappeared in the distance. Marjorie picked up her phone, "Morrison is that you". "Yes, was that the mysterious SUV?". "Yes". "hold on while I put a tail on it, Sergeant there's a Black Town car on the road leading from the Home, do me a favor and send up a drone to follow it and report back to me". "Yes Sir, it's done!" Morrison exited the SUV he waved to Marjorie and Martha opened the car door, waiting for them to leave the building, held the door open until they settled in, "OK Corporal, drive back to the Compound, we have work to do." The phone in the Car rang, "Morrison here". "Hey boss the SUV is no where to be found, we followed it for a few miles it turned west into a forested area and poof was gone". "Any large trucks in the area?". "Now that you mention it three or four trucks have emerged from the wooded area. Where the SUV disappeared, I will bet they drove it into the back of one of those trucks, did you have footage of the trucks, license plates?". "Will do a close up see if I can make out any of the licenses". "Corporal, keep surveillance on that road they may be setting up an ambush". "Will do Sir, I'll send a Squad to escort you to the Compound". "There's a parking area at Road Marker 136' I'll wait there for you, what's your ETA?" "About ten minutes." They pulled off onto the parking area and waited, a pickup Truck pulled in and there was the sound of machine gun fire. "What the, get down this SUV is armored, the Rangers should be here in a couple of minutes". "Morrison here, We are under fire, where in the hell are you?". "Driving into the Parking area I see the Hostiles, we are going Hot right now."

CHAPTER: FIFTY

The Ranger manning the machine gun on the Armored HUMVEE, opened fire and the tracers cut the Truck cab in half, the second burst imploded the gas tank, turning the truck into a ball of flame, the occupants spilled out of the Truck with their clothes in flames, screaming for help, "Grab an Fire Extinguisher and help those boys out make sure they are not armed, we need them alive so they can be questioned." The Corporal walked back to the HUMVEE with two of the attackers in tow, "Cuff these two they are to be charged with Terrorism and attempted murder." "What about the other two?". "Dead, one of them burned to a crisp the other with a bullet in his brain, quite a mess."

Sergeant Smith walked over to the SUV and opened the door. "Boss there is a second HUMVEE on the way we'll take point and the other HUMVEE will protect your rear." The convoy drove out onto the Highway and headed toward the Compound. "We should be there in a few minutes, Marjorie keep your eyes peeled for an ambush". "Morrison, you think they are planning to hit us a second time?" "I would bet on it, that attack was a ploy so we would drop our guard." Morrison called Sergeant Smith, "Sergeant, do we have a Drone available?". "Yes Sir, it is overhead as we speak" Morrison, "Driver, slow down have the Drone take point, I have a feeling that last attack was a feeler to check our strength. The real attackers are waiting for us to approach the Compound and I'm sure this time they will make sure they don't leave any witnesses, especially Martha Smithon." They were within two miles of the Compound, "Hey Sarge," There are three vans parkcd in the trees the Drone spotted the heat signatures from the engines". "Ok Morrison, we stop here." The words were not out of his mouth when he heard a loud "WOOSH" of an RPG being fired. "Backup, backup, we are under fire the attack is coming from two O'clock, they are in the tree line." The convoy backed up at top speed, "Do we have an armed Drone?" Roger that, Have target in sight "FIRE" before the enemy could react the woods where the Vans and hostiles were hidden erupted in a violent explosion, a Fire Ball rose up, the flames lighting up the sky and the outward force of the explosion incinerated the trees adding to the flames the vans melted killing the attackers instantly, as the smoke cleared a ten foot deep crater appeared. "Holy Smokes, I wouldn't want to be the target when one of those things strikes, BOOM all gone." Mrs. Smithon turned white, Marjorie laughed as she watched the blood drain from her face, "Well Martha it looks as if your Comrades aren't going to let you talk if they can help it, you must be a Encyclopedia of information about the Russian Secret Service." Mrs. Smithon, "I don't need any smart ass talk from you, what ever or whoever you are I did what I did to protect my country". "Smithon now you are expendable, your cover has been blown, your friends want you dead, when we get you to the Compound you will be safe. So sit back relax we will be there in a couple." When they arrived at the Compound a steel door that protected the underground parking area opened slowly, they drove into the underground and parked. Marjorie, "Have the Rangers made sure the underground hasn't been infiltrated." Lieutenant, "Recommend you stay in the SUV till we make sure the area is safe." The Lieutenant tapped on the car window, "All clear Captain Swift my people will escort you to the elevator". "Alright people lets go upstairs and get to work, Marjorie take Mrs. Smithon to the Room and wait for me. I will be in as soon as I file my report." Marjorie ushered Martha into a Sealed Room, it was lead lined there were no interior or exterior penetrations.

"We can start our Interview in here the room is sound proofed so your handlers cannot pick up any thing we say or whatever deal we work with you."

She made sure Martha Smithon was settled in, "Would you like a cup of coffee or tea?". "No thank you but a double Martini would be nice two olives, please." Marjorie, "Martha hand me your purse." She handed Marjorie her purse, she opened it and dumped the contents on the table and used a ruler to separated the items. "What are you doing young lady?". "Just making sure that there aren't any weapons, explosives or poison every thing in the purse will checked and if it passes muster will be returned. I am sure you would love to make us look like idiots, noticed you were wearing leather gloves, please remove them and lay them on the table." Marjorie picked them up and turned them inside out, "Well look at this, they have a special lining, may I have your hands please?" She took Martha's hands and placed her in cuffs and locked her to the steel bar welded to the table.

"What are you doing, am I under arrest? you can't treat me like a criminal."

"I'll be right back, I have to check on something."

Marjorie went into Morrison's office, "Morrison I think we have a problem". "She came in out of the cold way to easy, I think we should check the SUV she was in and strip search her, I have her cuffed to the bar a speak.

"Just a gut feeling that something isn't right." Morrison picked up the phone, "I need two women to strip search Martha Smithon, tell them to leave her cuffed to the bar, we feel she is up to no good". "It will take about an hour I have to call in people on standby". "Thanks, I could be totally wrong, but she could have shot me and escaped, instead she gives up and is in our inner-sanctum all cheery acting innocent." They ran the contents of her pocketbook through an x-ray scanner, the cigarette lighter was formed out of C4, the pen carried cyanide, they strip searched her and put her through a total scan.

Morrison handed the report to Marjorie, she slowly read the report, "I think, I can say you were right on, but now it looks like we found everything". "What about the SUV, found anything?". "OH Yes, a homing device, you were right about that to". "She sat there thinking, this has been to easy that bitch has something else up her sleeve. Where is she now?". "In the interrogation Room". "Is she cuffed?". "NO, we didn't see any reason". "What about her personal goods, her purse?". "She has it." Marjorie took off running, "Shut down the Room she's in and get her clothes and gloves out of there". "Why?" she has Anthrax in her gloves, she's going to introduce it into our air ducts it will contaminate the whole fucking building."

CHAPTER: FIFTY ONE

*J*ones had been Checking on the head of the school and the teachers to verify their backgrounds. The Head Master who was a woman had no history in the USA, and half the teachers were either Russian, Chinese or from the Ukraine the rest of the them had questionable credentials. He turned all the information over to Homeland Security and the FBI, "Director any information you can find on these people would be appreciated, they were running a spy school on American Soil". "Understand Agent Jones it will be on the top of my list". "Thank you Director."

Jones had spent the last two weeks researching the backgrounds of the students and a third of each class was trained in Spy Craft, one name that stood out was someone named James K. who was listed as an outstanding Spy Master, his basic role was to do whatever was necessary to bankroll the Organization, that would explain his expertise at scamming rich widows, robbing wealthy couples and placing the take in Off Shore Banks.

"I'll be a Son of a Bitch, this is all coming together, the School, Carl, Jimmy K., Nuclear Weapons, these Bastards are working to overthrow the Government."

Jones sent a memo to Morrison and Marjorie, "Have placed Jimmy K. as a student at the spy school, back about twenty years. It appears his job was to bankroll the Terrorists and help them buy weapons". "Oh, by the way how are the other Investigations proceeding?". "We are slowly but surely peeling the layers, this has been going on for years and years."

Jones decided to start interrogating the school Administrator and Teachers starting with the Head Mistress Lada Irina. He called Morrison, "I would like to start questioning everyone from the school, would you like to sit in?". "Yes, for the Head of the school, teachers the students that we know are being trained in Spy Craft. I'll leave it up to you who you want to be put under the scope". "Sounds good I'm going to work on the Head Mistress first." He sent a memo to the Head of Security, "Tomorrow at eight have Lada Irina in the interrogation room and make sure she is cuffed to the bar, thanks."

He was in the office at seven reviewing Lada's file, hopefully he would be able to flip her. She was sitting in the Interrogation Room at exactly eight in the morning at ten she started to complain, "What am I a slave?, you have no right to keep me chained up, I will sue." Jones walked into the Room at ten fifteen, "Miss Irina how are you?". "I have noting to say to you, I am being treated like a criminal I want to talk to the Russian Ambassador". "I am afraid that is not possible, you do not have Diplomatic Immunity and as there is no proof as to what is the country of your birth, I am afraid after we speak you will be tried as a Foreign Alien with no status, except as a Terrorist Spy, you will be sent to Gitmo or a Federal Prison for ten to twenty years."

"We have reviewed every one who has taught at the school, the students, what do you know about the student who goes by the name of James K.?, from your written correspondence you have been in touch with him a number of times in the last couple of years are you two related?"

Lada Irina, "I have no idea who you are speaking of I never heard the name."

Jones, "Really, from your letters I would say he is your first cousin, maybe your brother or better yet husband, come on we have his and your daughters DNA perfect match."

Her face flushed, and she shook her head vigorously, "Na, Na don't know him."

He placed a picture of Jimmy K. on the table and followed with a class photo with her standing next to him.

"Hell, you two graduated together and he's the father of your grown daughter, we have his DNA from a crime scene and your daughters from her College Dorm. How come your not married or are you?, and he just split leaving you with all the responsibility". "Have no idea what you are talking about, never met him and I have no daughter."

He walked to the door, "Hey Mike would you come in here, what is the scoop on Lada's daughter?"

Mike entered carrying a folder placing it on the table.

"This is a complete Dossier of a Elena Kamarovak she is a Chemistry Student at the local College."

Lada, "How did you obtain that information?"

"It is classified you have no need to know how we do anything, I think we should arrest her for espionage and bring her in for questioning."

Lada started to cry tearing at her hair, "No, No, I tell you whatever you want to know, leave my daughter alone". "OH, by the way Jimmy

K. has been paying for her tuition and we have proof that you have been in touch with her father just two days prior to us raiding the school. Now I am going to ask you again, where is he?"

She sat for a moment before she answered, "He was somewhere in Texas gathering more money for the cause, didn't say where but this was his last scam because the Police were getting too close."

"That's not going to cut it, I need the number of his cell phone and anything else you have on his location. I will slap your daughter in the slammer and unless you have a hundred thousand dollars for a lawyer she will stay locked up."

Jones slid a pad in front of her, "Write it all down and I want all the gory details how the school worked, what teachers are traitors, and students."

"Please, release my hands so I can write."

He sat there as if he was thinking about it, "NA, don't think that will happen, you can scribble and after we check out all your information if it checks out I'll let you commit suicide, that a deal?" She looked at him with hate in her eyes, "Your a no good bastard." He smiled, "I appreciate that, thank you, that's the nicest thing anyone has called me in a long time."

CHAPTER: FIFTY TWO

Morrison called Jones, "I am going to be kept busy for a few days questioning Susie, I heard through the grape vine you had our Miss Lada tearing her hair out, good very good. Talk to you in a couple of days." He scanned Susie's file for the second time, "How in the hell did she get clearance to this office, we have another sleeper, somebody was paid off to clear her or they just screwed up. I would tend to believe we have another sleeper, who paid someone for her clearance, so someone is on the take." He called Jones, "Can you send me a list of students at the school, we may have another sleeper working at the main office approving Agents clearances."

Two guards ushered Susie into Morrisons office, "Sit please we have an awful lot to talk about. You are one lucky lady, if it wasn't for me they would have killed you, I guess you knew too much, right now all I want to know is who approved your security clearance."

She sat there staring like a deer in the headlights.

"Hey Susie, I asked you a question who approved your security clearance". "I have no clue, why do you ask?"

"Just wondered how you were approved and how did you happened to be stationed here. Oh, by the way James K. says hello". "James, who I never heard of him?". "Was he your handler?". "Like I said never heard of him."

"Really, that's strange he went to the spy school for a year when you were a Sophomore. Sure you didn't meet him?"

She started to shake and stutter, "No, I am sure I didn't meet him, that is funny he says he knows you."

"Look, why don't you start talking it will go a lot easier on you if you tell us what your mission was and who your handler is". "I can't my baby". "Stop the shit you don't have any children, because you have never been pregnant, why don't you just tell the truth, if your butt is dropped in a Federal Prison your life span will be less than a week. We have enough on you to put you away for twenty years, the Bureau can give you a new identity, new name and a nice place to live think about it, they already tried to snuff you out once I'll guarantee there will be a second try this time they probably will succeed."

"I'll give you till tomorrow to decide, Guard take her to solitary and placed her under twenty four hour watch."

There was a knock on his office door, "Come in". "Boss she wants to see you". "Good, bring her in it's about time, did she give any clues as to what she had decided?". "None, all she said wanted to speak to you." Jones was sitting at his desk when she entered, "Sit down Susie, so what is your answer."

"I will tell you everything I know, but first I need everything in writing."

"I can do that and have the head of the Department approve and sign it."

Susie, "I can describe the person who approved my clearance, don't know her name she has an office in the Capital and works with a tall man, well built probably ex-soldier by his bearing."

"Describe the woman". "Asian, probably American born she didn't have any accent, well dressed, about five four. I could definitely recognize her and the man."

"Take her back to the cell and keep a fifteen minute watch." When she left Jones called his secretary, "Adel, please bring me that file on Susie and any other information we have on her case". "Yes sir". She laid it on his desk, "Anything else Sir?" "Not right now Adel, how about lunch around two?". "Sounds good Jonesy", she laughed and exited.

He opened the file and reviewed her Security paperwork, the signature read Jenny Franklin, and it was co-signed by a Colonel Brigham.

He picked up the phone, "Adel, can you please get me Security at the main office, I'll hold."

"Hello, Jenny Franklin, Agent Jones can I help you?" Jones, "Yes can you check a security clearance for Susie Smithon?, It was around ten years ago". "Hold on I'll be right back, let me look her up in the computer."

He waited holding the phone, leafing through the paperwork.

"I have the information do you want me to scan it to you?". "Yes that would be nice."

He clicked the computer and brought up the Security paper work, printed it out, checked who approved and signed the approval.

"There is something wrong with this, I can't quite put my finger on it."

Jones picked up a magnifying glass and checked the certifying stamp, it didn't look right. He took the copy to the lab.

"Hey Milt can you check out the seal on this Security paperwork something doesn't look right."

His phone rang, "What is it?". "The seal is forged someone in the main office appears to be selling false Security Clearances". "How in the Hell can a clerk in the Main office, get away with that?, it seems bazaar."

Jones hung up the phone, "She is playing a very dangerous game, didn't she think I would check, apparently not. I will say they are loyal to their cause, but the double talk makes no sense."

He sits back thinking, "They are keeping us guessing, because something is going to happen and they are setting the Department up for a fall."

CHAPTER: FIFTY THREE

He called in two guards, "Bring Susie to the Interrogation Room, before you take her out of solitary place her in leg irons and cuffs, when you put her in interrogation lock her to the bar, I don't want any screw ups she is extremely dangerous." The door to the Isolation Cell opened with a clang, she was half dozing the sound of the metal door hitting the wall startled her awake. "You woke me what is happening? Get the hell out of my cell that asshole music kept me up all night, need sleep."

"Lieutenant Jones wants to question you."

"It's three o'clock in the morning, tell him I'll talk to him in the morning."

"I don't think so, what Lieutenant Jones wants he gets. Sit still while I put on the leg irons and cuffs."

The second guard stood in the doorway watching as his partner kneels to place the chains around her ankles, before he can blink she wraps the chains around the guard who is attempting to place the leg irons around his neck there is a loud SNAP the sound of pain and surprise, "Oh god" as he turns blue and slumps to the cell floor as she pulls the leg chains tighter and smashes his face into the concrete. The second guard six foot two, two hundred and fifty pounds comes to life pulling his truncheon raises it to strike. The prisoner rolls to the left and grabs the dying guards Truncheon and strikes the standing guard between the legs with so much force that the only sound he can utter is a loud wheeze as he collapses on the floor writhing in pain. Susie as she steps over the writhing guard smashes his head with the truncheon, the force of the blows splatters his blood against the cell wall, "That will be the last time you fuck with little Susie" she exclaims smiling as she drops the truncheon and sprints down the prison corridor.

Jones is waiting in his office when the Alarm is sounded the doors in the prison cell close automatically. "What the hell is going on?", One of the other Agents stops at his office door, "A prisoner has escaped and killed two guards". "Who, killed what guards and who did you say escaped?". "Susie Smithon killed her guards and is loose somewhere in the Prison."

Jones, "I'll be a son of a bitch, I warned them she was dangerous. I knew she was playing me "Check Mate Susie, Check Mate."

His phone rang, "What, you want her dead or alive". "Does she have a gun?". "Not that I am aware of". "Be, careful it appears she is a trained Assassin". "I would like you to take her alive, but don't take any chances if necessary shoot to kill."

She had found an unlocked door to a storage room and out of breath closed and locked it behind her. She turned on the lights there on a shelve were neatly folded uniforms and cell phones.

Susie dropped her orange jump suit on the floor and put on a guards uniform, turned on the cell phone and listened to the chatter of the other guards.

"Where in the hell did she disappear to, they are bringing in a Company of Rangers to back us up. We are to stand down till they lock down the entire complex, then we are to systematically search every inch of the prison."

She ponders her next move, "Should I try to bluff my way or just make a break for it. I am sure the Rangers have orders to shoot to kill, they would love to hang my picture on their wall as a prize especially since I snuffed those two guards. The one asshole had it coming, he felt my ass and I crushed his stones."

Jones meets with Sergeant Smith and Colonel Bickford, "We have a Company of Rangers in place, the Compound is sealed and the rest of the Company will split up. Half up here and the rest will help search the prison." She slowly opened the door and peered down the hall, it was empty, she cautiously walks down the hall. "There's the bitch she was hiding in the storage room and changed into a guards uniform". "See I told you keep the prison clear she had to show sooner or later". "Sergeant we have her, what are your orders, capture or kill?". "Try to take her alive, but be extremely careful she might be five foot two or what ever but she is a Weapons Master be vigilant."

The Rangers systematically locked down and manually checked every door and cell in the Prison.

"We have her boxed in the West hallway."

Two Rangers approach Susie, "Halt, and lay down on the floor with your hands on top of your head, don't move or my partner will put a bullet in your head."

She did as ordered not saying a word, they cuffed her and placed leg irons on her ankles. She had her hands closed tightly.

Ranger, "Open your hands or I will break all your fucking fingers open them I am sure you don't want me to do that bitch."

She opened her hands and in her left hand she had a pick, in her right was a shive. "Damn, you are one slick lady, Private take off her jacket". "How?". "Get a pair of scissors."

"Stand up face the wall, I guarantee if you screw with me I will waste you. I am not some prison guard." He pushed her against the wall, "GOT IT". "Yes, Sergeant". "Good." The Sergeant phoned his Colonel, "I need a couple of female Rangers, she needs to be throughly searched to be safe I am sure she has something else up her sleeves."

After the Female Rangers stripped her down dressed her in a jump suit and chains, "Jake we found a Garrote, another knife and the cell phone had been sharpened to a razor on one edge and her shoes had C4 built into them." Jones, "Put her back into Solitary. I will think about how we will deal with her."

Six months later; Susies cell door opened, "Time for my two hours in the yard?" Female Guard, "You need a shower and a change of clothes, let's go the man wants to see you". "Really how nice of him I thought they forgot me in this shit hole." After the shower, change of clothes, a little spritz of perfume, the guard fluffed her hair. Replaced the leg irons and cuffs, "They want to see you in Interrogation, try to be civil Susie." To very large Rangers escorted her to be questioned. Locked her down and stood guard, "So what in the hell is going on, why am I here?" no answer from the Rangers. The door opened, Marjorie entered and sat facing the prisoner, "Susie I have an offer, you tell us what we want to know about the school, five years in prison, then you are deported to China. Susie, "Don't think so, the CCP will put my ass against a wall and shoot me or send me to the mines working me to death. I will tell you everything I know, five years and I am deported to Peru with a monthly stipend." Marjorie, "As long as your Intelligence is verified It's a deal, you attempt to escape or kill someone the deal is off. You will spend the rest of your life in Gitmo". "Understand."

CHAPTER: FIFTY FOUR

arjorie, "Shut down the air conditioning and reverse the blowers, that crazy bitch is trying to contaminate the the entire complex and kill us in the interim, get me a Hazmat Suit, quick." She was helped into the Suit, "Is anyone watching Martha?". "There is a guard watching her remotely, when was the last time he called in?" "It has been an hour, he is supposed to call every fifteen minutes". "Suit up the Strike Team and follow me, the Compound has been breeched." They started down the hall to the Interrogation Area. "Can you read any body temperatures, we may be walking into an ambush."

Marjorie, "Stop here, I will take point." She knelt down and crawled slowly down the hall, stopped to put on her Laser Enhancement Glasses, "I'll be a damned they have boobytrapped the hall, break the beam and "BOOM". Marjorie stops and signals the team to halt, she whispers. "The hall is boobytrapped, be careful of pressure plates. I say we back off, walk along the uncarpeted part of the floor."

When the entire Team had evacuated the area, Marjorie, "Sergeant have your men take a metal detector and check for plates under the rug and I need a floor plan of the lower level."

"Yes, Captain will do, Private you heard find a floor plan and you Corporal take a man and find a metal detector."

The Sergeant, "You two start removing the rug and be very careful I don't want any casualties." They cut the rug every five feet and slowly picked it up, carrying it out of the hall. "Stop there, wait for the metal detector and I need time to scan the floor plan, if I am correct somehow the exterior wall was penetrated, God knows how many Hostiles are waiting to suck us into a Box" Morrison calls Marjorie, "Marjorie what is your assessment of the situation". "The Compound has been compromised, I would stake my life on it that they have taken over the west wing on the lower level. Send a Squad of Rangers to seal the breach and another to cover the level above it. We have to keep them confined, if necessary we level the west wing." "Understand, I wonder what weapons they have? RPG's that are Nuclear Tipped, if they do we are in a world of shit, she may be right just level the west wing." The Rangers pulled an armored HUMVEE across the opening and the Sergeant sent a four man Reconnaissance Team to feel out the strength of the enemy.

"The rest of you men take up firing positions." There was the sound of machine gun fire and the Four Man Team retreated to safety. "Corporal, have the men take up firing positions when they are in position fire at will." The Rangers poured fire into the breach in the wall, "Private, man the RPG and fire into the building", there was a loud whoosh and then a loud explosion, "Again", he fired a second RPG and after the explosion there are screams of pain. "Now, smoke grenades and tear gas, they didn't think we would fire on them while they occupy the West wing", He called his men in the Building, "Corporal shunt the elevator and have a team take the stairs, use smoke grenades, then phosphorus grenades". "But Sergeant aren't they illegal when used against civilians?". "They are armed Hostiles and Terrorists, so do as I say put a few well placed rockets down the stair well, if we can't drive them out of the lower level I have orders to demolish the West Wing." He no sooner finished the call and the building was rocked with a number of explosions, the smell of phosphorus and people shrieking in pain, he looked up and out of the hole screaming was a human torch, "Duck for cover the bastard is loaded with ammo and grenades, he's looking to take us out."

One of the Rangers stands up and fires point blank center mass, emptying his weapon into the attacker. The bullets cause the ammo and grenades to explode the force of the explosion lifted the HUMVEE off the ground knocking the Rangers off their feet and raining human remains on everyone and everything.

"Goddamned, frigging mess, go get the bastards before they have a chance to recover" Sarge here, "Storm the cell area, we need to occupy the offices, but be aware I don't want anyone killed by friendly fire."

"I hear you Sarge no friendly fire."

Two four man teams entered the building, one team entered the left wing and the other the right.

"A-Team any hostiles not yet, we just counted six dead and three wounded, how about B-Team?"

"So far this sector appears to be negative." "Be careful, it could be an ambush, and keep a look out there is a Team advancing from the first floor, the Password is Alpha Diana."

A-Team heard automatic fire from the left, the Squad Leader called for backup, "Sarge, we need someone to cover our back we don't have enough manpower to cover our rear they could be waiting to attack our flank."

"Understand, Corporal send in another four man team to cover "A" and "B" teams backs to make sure they aren't flanked."

"Who goes there, give the password?". "Team C, password is Alpha Diana.". "Is that you Lieutenant, yes Corporal have you encountered any Hostiles?". "No Sir, this area appears clear we found a number of bodies and some wounded, otherwise no resistance, there is the sound of automatic fire from the left where B Team is located."

"OK, sweep the area, and lock it down. I'm heading to the cell to see if our Susie is still locked up or they broke her out." The Lieutenant, you two setup a machine gun to cover the stairwell, Team A backtrack to make sure this area is cleared. "I'll take six men and relieve the pressure on Team B to make sure there are no more surprises." The Cell was open and the prisoner missing,"Where in the hell could she be?". "I have no idea, her cover has been blown so she is really no good to them." B Team Leader, "Area cleared, all insurgents eliminated." Sergeant Smith, "Morrison area cleared, location of prisoner unknown."

CHAPTER: FIFTY FIVE

Marjorie "I Just had Martha Smithon and Lada Irina the Schools Head Mistress transferred to the Federal Prison, we are still searching for Susie, she has to be somewhere in the Compound." Morrison, "I want you and Sergeant Smith to do a sweep of the lower level, take two squads and find her."

Marjorie called Sergeant Smith into the map room, "She must still be somewhere in the Compound" she laid a blueprint of the building on the table, "This lower section was built on an existing foundation and there is a large storm drain under the West wing, if the Attackers knew about this they are planning on using it as an escape route. That's why we found so few enemy casualties, all we captured were four prisoners the rest have vanished into thin air. Send a squad into the storm drain maybe they can smoke out any stragglers."

"There is a manhole one quarter mile from the building, it is close to a dirt road, Sarge do we have any Drones or better send a Chopper we can use to get eyes on the site?"

"I'll check, if there is a Drone we can send up". "It may be to late, they could have already escaped."

"They are probably running dark, make sure the Drone has a heat sensor, hopefully they haven't exited the dirt road and are on the main highway, because we will have a hell of a time getting a fix on them."

The Drone flew over the backroad, the Controller, "So far I haven't been able to get a fix on the Enemies vehicles, there appears to be bodies around the manhole, but be careful they may be boobytrapped, when you roll the body over it pulls out the pin on a grenade and BOOM."

Sergeant Smith, "How many people do we have searching the Storm Drains". "A four man Team", "Get them back, I would bet the exit to the drain is set to blow the minute they raise the lid, and they will be toast", "Corporal over, can you hear me? withdraw do not complete mission, believe area is mined."

"No, answer they must be in a dead zone." "Get someone down there and warn them, now."

"Abrams, move don't let the Team open the Storm Hatch, it probably has been wired."

"Yes Sergeant, I'm on my way."

Abrams entered the tunnel and started running, "Corporal pullback the hatch has been wired, damned this garbage." He spotted a flashlight in the distance, and hollered, "Corporal, stop the mission is canceled."

The flashlight stopped moving, "Halt, do not advance." "Corporal, it's Private Abrams, mission canceled the tunnel is a trap."

"What's the password, "Alpha Diane", now stop, the exit is wired to blow when you open it."

"Roger that, OK men lets go back to the Compound, we'll have to check out the area from topside."

Marjorie, "Do we have a Chopper up? Yes Captain, it is doing surveillance on the Highway, we think they were driving a couple of pickup trucks."

"I say we put up roadblocks North and South and stop all traffic, maybe we can get them to do something stupid, like run for it, try to shoot it out, we need to take a prisoner and get him or her to talk."

"Copter here, I think I spotted one of the trucks it has a machine gun mounted in the bed of the truck, with two men manning it. If they wanted they could slaughter all the motorists on the road, we need to be careful how they are approached."

The Copter flew low overhead and started to signal the traffic behind the truck to slow down, by shining a light into the windshields. The front drivers looked up and immediately started to slow allowing the truck to advance a quarter mile ahead. "Ok, they are almost to the roadblock, we have detoured all traffic on the opposite lane, be aware they are fully armed" Driver of escaping truck, "Holy Shit, there's a roadblock ahead, what now?". "We run the blockade". "Are you nuts. "Driver, The truck is armor plated with bulletproof glass, they can't stop us." He hit the gas the truck was clipping along at one hundred miles an hour as they approached the roadblock. Lieutenant, "Hold your fire, I'll tell you when to shoot." The Lieutenant held up his hand, "Every one use armor piercing ammo, when I drop my hand fire at will." His hand dropped gave the order, "Now, take those bastards out." The Sniper took aim his rifle was loaded with armor piercing tracers, he looked through the scope aimed at the driver took a deep breath and pulled the trigger he watched through the scope saw the drivers look of surprise as the bullet pierced the windshield and penetrated his forehead, blowing his brains all over the inside of the truck cab and killing his partner sitting behind him in the back seat. The Terrorist sitting in the passenger seat attempted to take control of the steering wheel, but to late the truck was traveling at such a speed it careened to the left striking the concrete barrier, the truck rolled over throwing the two men sitting in the truck bed manning the machine gun onto the blacktop, the second round hit the gas tank causing the truck to implode, there was a blinding flash and the truck disintegrated. Sergeant, "What in the hell was that?". "The truck must have been loaded with C4, one of them on the blacktop is moving, you two see if he is breathing be careful he can still be dangerous and that truck is roaring hot."

They rolled the survivor over the left side of his face where he had landed was hamburger. "He's barely breathing". "Pick him up and drag him back to the Ambulance."

Martha had been rescued by the attackers, the guards throat had been slit, she was escorted through a rear exit. She was taken to an Armored SUV, the driver drove south, "You are free Comrade, the Major wants to give you Royal Cross for service to the Father Land." Martha, "Where are we going?". "To airport there is a private jet waiting." The SUV was parked in a hanger, the door closed, "Come Martha the Major is waiting, you need to be debriefed". "Comrade please sit, How much did you tell the Capitalist?". "Nothing, they are fools I would never betray the cause." She was questioned far into the night, "Sergeant take our Comrade Martha to the plane, we must be out of the country before daylight. The plane took off at one pm, when they were in neutral airspace, Major, "Sergeant it's time, she cannot be trusted I am sure she is a double agent." One of the soldiers sat in the seat behind Martha, pulled out a Garrote the Major sitting facing her reached over holding her arms while the Garrote was placed around her throat and pulled tight she was strangled, "Open the bay door." Her body floated down and down.

CHAPTER: FIFTY SIX

"We found Susie hiding under a stair way begging for her life, what do you want us to do with her?" Jake, "For now throw her into Solitary and tell her I am tired of her lies and the Feds are sending her for the rest of her life to Guantanamo, because there is a belief she has no relevant information to give us concerning who the mole is inside the our Organization, no matter what she says let her stew for a week. I only want Rangers to guard her, do you understand? because if I find out they have been replaced you Corporal and whoever else is involved will be court marshaled and sent to Leavenworth, I guarantee it."

"Yes Sir, I understand Sir, Rangers to guard her, yes sir." "Don't just stand looking at me Corporal do it."

Marjorie calls Morrison, "We have a hit on someone trying to send money to that offshore bank that is part of the Cartel, it originates out of Houston, what do you want me to do?"

"Tell our man at the bank,to tell Jimmy K. they are having trouble transferring the money at this time, they will hold it in the bank account and he will have to come in tomorrow morning and the bank will complete the transfer at that time. Have him take a picture of Jimmy K.,have the bank send it to us for verification."

"Will do, now what?". "We fly there and apprehend our boy Jimmy in the morning or maybe tonight, can't let him slip through our fingers after all this time. Anything on Henry?". "Now that you mention it our algorithm has picked up what appears to be his calling card in the Houston area.". "Good, maybe we can kill two fish at the same time."

Henry was sitting at his computer trying to lure someone into his trap, when the door to the apartment slammed open. "Henry, you are one big asshole, I told you not to start trying to lure women until this scam is over, then you can do whatever." Henry just sat there thinking, "I am of no use to this Organization and I get a creepy feeling down my back that my boy Jimmy has been given the orders to get rid of me." Jimmy, "Sorry Buddy, didn't mean to blow off like that what say we go for a beer?"

"Sure Jimmy, sounds great give me a couple of minutes to change my clothes and we can go."

Henry walked into the bedroom shut the door, he reached under the bed and pulled out the Glock, two clips, a small pistol and a hunting knife. Placed one in the holster behind his back, the other in his leg holster and the knife in a sheath on the other leg, put a form fitting bullet proof vest under the his shirt, concealed it with a long coat. Henry looked in the mirror. "I don't think my boy will suspect anything, he thinks I'm just here to be used,I have big news for him." He exited the bedroom, "Well bud let's go get a few drinks."

The private jet landed at two in the morning, Morrison, "Do we still have eyes on them?" Jones, "Yes, have two Agents tailing them twenty four hours, I have an FBI Swat Team ready to go we want to arrest both of them alive at the same time."

Henry, hey Jimmy I have to take a piss I'm going to the head be right back. He slipped out of the back door of the bar and hailed a cab. "Where's the nearest Cat House?" Cab Driver, "That will cost you a pineapple(50 dollar bill)". "No problem", the Cab Driver dropped him off in front of at the House, Henry slipped him a fifty. Jimmy was sitting at the bar waiting for Henry to return from the Head, "Where did the little Dick disappear to?" he left the bar and opened the bathroom door, it was empty no Henry. "That little bastard screwed, enough of this I'm going back to the apartment." He will get his tonight when he's asleep, I'll use a pillow to muffle the sound when I put a bullet in his head, he'll never know what hit him. Jimmy opened the apartment door and crashed on the couch, opened a beer was relaxing when the door to the apartment was blown off the hinges he was surrounded by masked men pointing automatic weapons at his head, before he could think they had him prone on the floor, placing cuffs on him and leg irons on his ankles. Jones and Morrison entered and read him his rights, "We have a Federal Warrant for your arrest, you are being charged with money laundering, aiding and abetting a terrorist organization, and attempted murder." Morrison, "Where is Henry?" Jimmy "I haven't a clue, probably at a Cat House I'm not his baby sitter he's over twenty one," "Take him away and put him in a holding cell, Henry can't be far we'll track his ass down before the nights over." Henry, "I need to spent a couple of hours being pleasured at the Cat House, it was two in the morning when Henry walked into the House and went to the desk. He looked around, feeling something wasn't quite right. Out of the shadows appears a Gorilla about six four, three hundred pounds, he growled, "CAN I HELP YOU?" Yea a cabbie dropped me off said I could have a good time here." "Sure thing have just the right girl for you, go up to room 202 and wait there, she'll be right up." Henry walked up the stairs entered Room 202 thinking, "This place is a set up," he glanced around for a way out, looked out the window and spied a fire escape, he tried to open the window but it wouldn't budge.

Picked up a chair and smashed the glass as he started to climb out on the fire escape, the Gorilla entered the room and charged Henry. He instinctively pulled the Glock out of the holster and fired three times hitting the charging attacker center mass, he stopped a couple of feet from where Henry stood with a surprised look on his face falling forward screaming, "I will kill you, you little fucker." Henry jumped, onto the fire escape to keep from being crushed by the now dead attacker. He could hear sirens in the distance, "My ass is grass unless I get the hell out of here." Marjorie, "Morrison I'm on my way to a shooting the description of the shooter matches Henry, I may need backup." Morrison, "I'll send two of the Team to your location, be careful." Marjorie enters the house, "Federal Officer, what is the location of the shooter?". "Second floor room 202, I heard three gun shots." She ran up the stairs and entered the room, there hanging half way out the window was one big dude and from the look of him was dead as hell, and no sign of Henry.

"I don't believe this shit he slipped through my fingers again, I can't let that little bastard escape." She looked out the smashed window Henry was gone. Marjorie, "Morrison, put out a BOLO on Henry, that creep just killed the bouncer he has to be somewhere in the area." Henry headed for the Yacht Basin, he spotted a Yacht being loaded it was getting ready for a long cruise. Henry walked up to the Second Mate, "Hey Mate, looking for a deck hand? I am willing to do what ever is necessary." Second, "If you don't mind it's a long voyage to the West Indies". "Sounds good to me, when do we leave?". "This morning at three". "You have to get your gear". "No need I'm good, just show me where my bunk is." One of the crew showed him where he was to bunk, "Breakfast is at six, Henry laid down," Now I have to find how to get the hell out of West Indies rolled over going to sleep. The FBI Swat Team scoured the entire neighborhood, "No Henry," he disappeared. Morrison and Marjorie stood looking out to sea, Marjorie, "Damned look at that Yacht heading out to sea, what a life maybe someday I'll have my own boat." His phone rang, "Yes, you are serious? that sucks, Marjorie the FBI wants you placed under house arrest. They say your Investigation is still ongoing and until it is completed you have to wear an Ankle Monitor". "Kiss my ass, are they for real? the FBI is taking forever to complete the investigation I'll be a hundred years old by the time they finish." Morrison, "Afraid so, I will do everything possible to get you cleared, so please just go with the flow."